'I have no ta...
night stands.'

Jake laughed wi...
exactly what I had ...

'Oh? And what *did* you have in mind?'

'No, I don't think this is quite the right moment to explain. Why didn't you tell me who you were?'

'I don't think this is quite the right moment to explain,' Georgia countered crisply. 'I'm sorry about the misunderstanding with the security people—I hope your injuries aren't serious?'

'I'll live,' he returned, an inflection of sardonic humour in his voice as he cautiously felt his swollen eye.

'I'll ask the kitchen to send you up a raw steak.'

'You could try kissing it better…?'

Her blue eyes flashed him a frost warning. 'I'll ask the kitchen to send up a raw steak,' she reiterated dampeningly.

Jake chuckled with wry amusement. 'You know, you should always wear diamonds,' he remarked in lazy mockery. 'They go with your eyes.'

Susanne McCarthy grew up in South London but she always wanted to live in the country, and shortly after her marriage she moved to Shropshire with her husband. They live in a house on a hill with lots of dogs and cats. She loves to travel—but she loves to come home. As well as her writing, she still enjoys her career as a teacher in adult education, though she only works part-time now.

Recent titles by the same author:

FORSAKING ALL OTHERS

BAD INFLUENCE

BY
SUSANNE McCARTHY

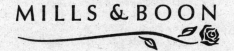

MILLS & BOON

*All the characters in this book have no existence outside the imagination
of the author, and have no relation whatsoever to anyone bearing the
same name or names. They are not even distantly inspired by any
individual known or unknown to the author, and all the incidents are
pure invention.*

*MILLS & BOON and the Rose Device
are trademarks of the publisher.
Harlequin Mills & Boon Limited,
Eton House, 18-24 Paradise Road, Richmond, Surrey TW9 1SR*

© Susanne McCarthy 1996

ISBN 0 263 79842 9

*Set in Times Roman 10 on 11¼ pt.
01-9612-62926 C1*

Made and printed in Great Britain

CHAPTER ONE

'MARRY you? Don't be ridiculous!' Georgia Geldard's blue eyes had more than once been likened to polar ice, and they had never been more frosty than at this moment. 'And if you think I'm going to consent to spending one single night on this yacht, you can just think again,' she added on a note of withering scorn.

Unfortunately her sharp words served only to provoke her captor into a display of pure Latin machismo. 'But, *querida*, you have no choice.' He swaggered with over-stated arrogance. 'I can see that you have no weapons concealed about your person...'

Georgia felt a faint blush of pink rise to her cheeks. She was acutely conscious that the brief blue silk bikini concealed very little; if only she had at least paused to slip on a shirt or something before accepting César's seemingly innocent invitation. The trouble was, she had known César Nunez de Perez since he was a lanky adolescent whose only interest was American baseball, and she still thought of him as a mere boy, so when he had zoomed up beside her yacht on his latest toy—a jet-ski—she had quite readily agreed to lay aside the very dull report on world coffee production she had been studying and go for a ride with him. And when he had suggested that they step aboard his yacht for a cool drink she had thought nothing of it. She would never have trusted a grown man in such circumstances.

But though he was now an extremely spoiled and self-important young man of twenty-two, she had no intention of letting him intimidate her. 'Oh, for goodness' sake, César, stop playing silly games,' she rapped impatiently. 'Tell your captain to take us back to Mangrove Bay at once.'

César's handsome young face took on a sulky pout. 'But, Georgia, you know how I feel about you,' he pleaded. 'I adore you—I worship at your feet.'

'I have no desire at all to be worshipped,' she retorted. 'Besides, don't you think you're a little too old for that sort of adolescent infatuation?'

'Infatuation?' Oh, dear—she had affronted his fragile dignity again. 'You call it that? I offer to marry you— no less! You cannot think me a fortune-hunter—my father is an extremely wealthy man, as you well know. As my wife, you would enjoy the highest status and privilege...'

'I'm quite happy with the status I have, thank you. And being chief executive of one of the most successful companies in Europe is privilege enough for anyone.'

'But is no life for a woman!' he protested heatedly. 'It is not good that you should be all the time concerning yourself with business affairs—it is not natural. I do not know what your grandfather could have been thinking of, to leave such a responsibility to you.'

'He was thinking very wisely, as he always did,' she countered, with brusque disregard for his sensibilities. 'I was trained to run the Geldard Corporation from my cradle. I enjoy it, and I'm damned good at it. And I intend to go on doing it for the next fifty years, if I live that long! And, what's more, I have no intention of marrying anyone—least of all you. That you could stoop to kidnapping me...!'

The handsome boy lifted his magnificently developed shoulders in a dismissive shrug, though two betraying spots of colour darkened his cheeks. 'A little trick...'

'A *little* trick? Is that what you call it?' Those blue eyes flashed with cold fire. 'You lure me aboard your yacht by the most underhand means; you lock me in...'

'It was... how you say? An impulse,' he argued fervently. 'I had not planned. But I saw you there on your boat, so beautiful, like a golden goddess shimmering in the sunlight. It brought to my head a fever...'

'Well, you should have taken an aspirin,' she retorted dampeningly. 'Now, will you please take me back to Mangrove Bay?'

He shook his head. 'I cannot do that, *mi querida*,' he insisted, his voice throbbingly low. 'I would treat you with all honour, I swear it. If you would but be sensible, I would make you at once my bride. But if you will persist in this obstinacy, you leave me no choice. Once I have you in my bed, I will make love to you until you have no more will to resist me...'

Georgia decided on a strategic retreat behind a large onyx coffee-table—the yacht was furnished with somewhat flamboyant taste. 'Listen, César,' she coaxed, trying to throw the cold water of reason over his theatricals, 'you really don't want to marry me. Apart from anything else, I'm nearly six years older than you...'

'Your age is immaterial to me!' he protested ardently. 'Besides, you do not look so old.'

'Thank you,' she responded with dry amusement. 'But I don't imagine your father would be very pleased. I'm sure he would prefer for you to marry some nice, sweet girl of your own age, who would adore you and give you lots and lots of beautiful babies.'

'My father does not dictate to me,' he protested sulkily. 'Besides, how could I even think of marrying my stupid cousin, when it is you I adore?'

Georgia smiled in gentle understanding. 'So he *has* got someone lined up for you,' she mused. 'You wouldn't be very wise to defy him, you know. What would you do if he cut you off without a penny?'

'I would not care!'

'No?' She lifted one delicately arched eyebrow in cool enquiry. 'Even though it would then mean that *I* would be the one to hold the purse-strings? I don't think you'd like that very much, César.'

He coloured in anger. 'It would not be so!' he insisted fiercely. 'In my household I would be the master. I would teach you to obey me!'

Her eyes flashed him a look of sardonic humour. 'Oh, really? At the same time as worshipping at my feet?'

Recognising that he was in danger of coming off worst in the argument, the young man retreated into a display of affronted dignity. 'I will give you a little longer to consider my offer,' he declared loftily. 'I am sure you will come to recognise the wisdom of accepting my proposal—as night-time approaches.' And, sweeping magnificently out of the state-room, he closed the door behind him—and locked it.

Left alone, Georgia sighed with wry impatience. What a ridiculous situation to find herself in, with that silly boy imagining himself to be in love with her—it would be laughable if it wasn't such a damned nuisance. Oh, she was quite certain that even in his present temper César would stop short of actually assaulting her, but she really didn't have time to hang around waiting for him to come to his senses.

However well-trained and discreet her staff, her disappearance—in broad daylight, from the deck of her own yacht in the safety of one of Bermuda's most exclusive hide-away resorts—was not something that could be hushed up for long. There would be all sorts of speculation, which could have a very destabilising effect on Geldard's shares—it was a risk she couldn't afford to take.

Over on the starboard beam, she could see that they would soon be rounding Spanish Point, leaving the island-dotted haven of the Great Sound behind; the powerful yacht would be able to pick up speed as they headed out for open water—across the vast, empty miles of the legendary Bermuda Triangle towards South

America. If she was going to escape, it was going to have to be right now.

Most of the windows were sealed units, except for two of the rear ones which served as emergency exits. It was typical of César, she reflected with a trace of wry amusement, that in making his dramatic gesture of locking her in he had forgotten such a critical detail. Slanting a swift glance at the locked door, she knocked up the catch of one of the windows and slipped nimbly out onto the narrow gunwale that ran along the side of the boat.

The blue water churning beneath her seemed to be racing by awfully fast, and for a brief moment she felt a little giddy. But she quickly regained her balance and edged her way to the stern, crouching low to avoid being seen from the bridge. If she remembered rightly, there was an inflatable tender at the stern of the yacht, similar to her own—if she could launch that without being seen, she ought to be able to paddle ashore. It would be a risk, of course—she wasn't sure of the currents—but they couldn't be much more than a thousand yards from land.

To her relief, the tender was where she had expected it to be. Keeping her fingers crossed that no one would be watching aft, she dragged the small dinghy to the rail and swung it over. No one raised the alarm as it bobbed away in the wake, not much bigger than a truck tyre. Stepping carefully over the rail, she launched herself after it in a long dive that took her well clear of the danger of the yacht's twin propellors.

She was a strong swimmer—a mile in the morning before breakfast in the pool at her Berkshire home was her regular exercise. Striking out in a powerful breast-stroke, she reached the dinghy in a few minutes. It was no easy task to scramble up into the frail craft but she managed it, and then, using the late afternoon sun to give her an estimate of due south, she began to paddle for the shore.

It was hard to guess how deep the water was here—it was so clear that she could see the myriad schools of tiny fish darting across the sandy bottom. But there was coral, too—she would have to be careful to avoid jagging the bottom of the dinghy on its razor-sharp edges. Kneeling up in the bottom of the dinghy, she could only catch an occasional glimpse of the shore as she crested a wave. It seemed to be getting no nearer, but at least there was no sign of pursuit...

A warning horn blared urgently, and a gleaming white hull sheered past almost above her; the helmsman must have taken expert last-minute avoiding action, slewing the yacht around to avoid a collision, but the churning wake chopped into the flimsy dinghy, tossing it aside like so much flotsam.

The paddle flew out of her hand and she hit the water with an impact that knocked all the breath out of her. Half-dazed, she went under, choking as she fought blindly in the swirling undercurrent, desperate to find the surface. Her lungs were hurting and there was a buzzing sound in her ears... She could feel herself growing heavier, her limbs no longer under her control. She wouldn't let herself drown... She *wouldn't*...

'Relax, Blondie—I've got you.'

A strong arm had slipped around her waist, lifting her to the surface, and she gasped thankfully for air, her head tipping back against a broad, solid shoulder. Exhausted, she could only dimly register that it certainly wasn't César, nor any of his South American crew, who had come to her rescue. The accent was unmistakably, uncompromisingly Australian.

She closed her eyes in relief, letting him tow her through the water to the side of the yacht. As if from a great distance she heard her rescuer giving orders, and then she was hauled unceremoniously up onto the deck and felt the welcome comfort of a blanket being wrapped around her. And then someone lifted her as if she weighed no more than a feather, and carried her along the deck and into a cabin.

She was lowered onto a deep, well-padded sofa and she let her head fall back with a sigh. 'Thank you,' she murmured with heartfelt gratitude.

A deep, mocking laugh answered her. 'Don't mention it. The pleasure, I assure you, was all mine.'

She opened her eyes quickly, regarding her rescuer with some misgiving. He was big, and handsome in a disconcertingly rugged way. His hair, darkened now by the sea, would probably be almost blond, and cut rather longer than convention dictated—at present it curled in damp tendrils over his ears. His eyes were a shade somewhere between brown and hazel, deep-set beneath straight dark brows. And he was wearing only a towel, slung low around his waist.

Her heart gave a thud of alarm; had she escaped from the frying pan only to fall into a very much more dangerous fire? Of course—she tried desperately to rationalise—he had just dragged her out of the water; he would have had to take his wet clothes off... She closed her eyes again swiftly, but the image of that darkly bronzed body, hard-muscled and covered with a smattering of rough, male hair, seemed to have been burned onto her eyelids.

'Brandy?' he offered, a sardonic inflection in his voice.

'Er... No, thank you...'

'You'd better drink it.'

Her eyes flew open in angry indignation as he sat down on the edge of the sofa beside her, sliding his arm around her shoulders to lift her to a sitting position. A strong whiff of alcohol assailed her nostrils, and as she opened her mouth to protest he deftly tipped the fiery liquid down her throat.

She gasped in shock, choking as she swallowed it. 'How...*dare* you?' she demanded, furious.

'I don't want you catching pneumonia on me,' he taunted in that laconic Australian drawl. 'That would rather spoil the game.'

She glared up at him, the heat of the unfamiliar brandy coursing through her veins and doing odd things to the rate of her heartbeat. This was clearly a man who was accustomed to having his every word unquestioningly obeyed; there was an arrogance in that strongly carved face that would make poor César look positively meek.

He lifted one questioning eyebrow. 'What's wrong, Blondie? Aren't I playing it to the right script?'

She hesitated, struggling to get a grip on the situation. She wasn't accustomed to being treated with such off-hand familiarity. Brought up by her grandfather with the knowledge of the substantial fortune she was to in-herit, she had been taught from her cradle to keep any hint of emotion under the strictest control, and the image of chilling reserve she projected was usually enough to keep the world at arm's length.

'I...appreciate your rescuing me,' she managed, her voice stiff with dignity. 'However, I would prefer it if you didn't call me Blondie.'

He shrugged those wide shoulders in a gesture of casual unconcern. 'OK—so what do you want me to call you?'

She slanted him a measured glance from beneath her lashes. He didn't know who she was. That wasn't sur-prising, really—she was usually quite successful in avoiding having her picture in the papers, and even if he had seen it he was unlikely to recognise her with her hair soaking wet and slicked to her head.

Well, that suited her. She had no idea who he was either—she might easily find herself in a far more dangerous position than with César. 'I...there's no need for you to call me anything,' she responded as coolly as she could. 'If you would just be so kind as to take me back to Mangrove Bay...'

He laughed that lazy, mocking laugh. 'Don't put on that haughty act with me,' he advised drily. 'You're not the first pretty mermaid to get herself washed up alongside my boat. Though I have to admit,' he added, slanting her a look of insolent approval, 'you're the best looker of the bunch so far.'

She stared up at him in shocked amazement. 'You surely don't believe I did that deliberately?'

'Either that or you're plumb crazy,' he returned, a glint of amusement in those dark, deep-set eyes. 'You don't look stupid enough to take a flimsy thing like that out for a pleasure cruise, and it'd be a pretty bizarre way to commit suicide.'

'I certainly wasn't trying to commit suicide!' she protested hotly.

'Then what *were* you doing?'

'I—' She stopped herself abruptly; she couldn't tell him the truth without revealing who she was—and worse, revealing details of the awkward episode with César. 'I don't even know who you are,' she countered, injecting several degrees of frost into her voice.

'No?' He was *laughing* at her! 'You mean any old yacht would have done? Provided it was big enough and swanky enough, of course. Well, I guess that puts me in my place.'

She glanced around, for the first time properly taking stock of her surroundings. The yacht certainly was 'swanky', although the style was as uncompromisingly masculine as the owner. The saloon was easily as large as her own. Rich dark mahogany lined the walls, and the huge, comfortable sofa she was lying on was one of four, upholstered in pale cow-hide, surrounding a heavy brass-edged coffee-table. Beyond, she could see a dining area that would easily seat twelve around a large oval table.

'Who *are* you?' she queried, frowning up at him.

'Allow me to introduce myself.' A disturbingly sensual smile was curving that sardonic mouth. 'Jackson Morgan—at your service. My friends call me Jake.'

Jake Morgan—oh, damn, that was all she needed! Jake Morgan was known as one of the most predatory sharks of the southern hemisphere. His name had first hit the financial pages only about five or six years ago, but in that short time he had earned himself a reputation for gobbling up smaller fry apparently just for the sake of it.

And he was as famous in the tabloids as he was in the serious financial press, she had heard—his reputation with women was deadly. She had been inclined to doubt a good many of the stories about him, knowing how fond the newspapers could be of exaggeration—but now that she had met him she could believe every one.

'Ah, so the name does mean something to you after all?' he taunted, his eyes glinting with dark humour. 'Are those dollar signs I see lighting up those great big beautiful eyes? What were you hoping for? A couple of weeks cruising in the sun and a few pretty diamonds to take home with you afterwards? Or something more? I wonder if you'd be worth it...?'

Before she had time to realise what he was going to do, he had bent his head and his mouth had brushed lightly over hers. She felt the heat, and her lips parted in shock; only once before had anyone ever presumed to kiss her like this—she had been seventeen years old, and he had got her riding crop across his cheek for his insolence.

But this was alarmingly different. As the moist tip of his tongue flickered into the sensitive corners of her lips she felt an odd little shimmer of heat run through her veins. The musky scent of his skin, mingled with the salt tang of the sea, was somehow drugging her senses, making her heart beat so fast that it was difficult to breathe.

She closed her eyes, a strange melting sensation flowing through her as he pinned her back against the warm leather upholstery, yielding helplessly as he plundered the soft sweetness of her mouth in a flagrantly sensual exploration. Maybe it was just the brandy that was making her head float like this...

He lifted his head, and she opened her eyes to find him looking down at her in quizzical amusement. 'That's quite an act, Blondie,' he commented, a mocking edge in his voice. 'Shiver, then sizzle—you could make a man catch something far worse than pneumonia.'

Shock turned to coruscating anger, and without thinking about it she swung her hand at his cheek. Her palm sang and he gasped in surprise, touching his fingertips to the scarlet mark she had made. And then his eyes darkened with lethal anger, and with swift ruthlessness he had grasped both her wrists, forcing them down behind her back and pinioning them with one powerful hand.

'So you like to play rough, do you?' he grated menacingly. 'Well, I can play a great deal rougher than you, and I can assure you that you'll be the one who comes off worst.'

The kiss he inflicted on her was pure punishment, his lips crushing hers apart, his plundering tongue swirling deep into her mouth, asserting his mastery. She struggled wildly but she couldn't escape—he was far too strong for her and she was only hurting herself. When at last he lifted his head, his mocking laughter inflamed her fury.

'Let me go!' she raged fiercely. 'How dare you treat me like this?'

'Well, now, isn't this what you were after, frolicking around my boat?' he sneered with icy contempt. 'Why waste time playing coy little games? Like I said, you're not the first pretty mermaid to try that kind of trick to get herself on board, but you're the first who's gone to such bold extremes.'

As he spoke, and his eyes raked coolly down over her body, the blanket had fallen away, and with a sudden stab of horror she realised that her bikini had gone—leaving her completely naked. It had been just a flimsy thing, designed for lounging around in the sun rather than serious swimming, and in her floundering around in the water it must have come unfastened without her even noticing. A deep blush of humiliation suffused her cheeks, and she turned her face away from him in total defeat.

'Hey, what's this?' The harshness was suddenly gone from his voice. With a gentle hand he turned her face back towards him, brushing away a tear that sparkled on her cheek. She gazed up into those fathomless dark eyes, feeling herself once again drowning...

And then abruptly he let her go, rising to his feet and tossing the blanket back over her in a gesture of scornful disdain. 'OK, Blondie—you get the Oscar for that one. I don't know what game you're playing but it's a new one on me, and until I know the rules you can deal me out.'

Still dazed with shock, she wrapped the blanket around herself, curling herself up into a defensive ball on the sofa, warily watching his every move.

'And spare me the Sarah Bernhardt impersonation,' he rapped acidly. 'It won't wash. Just get your cute little backside through that door and find yourself something to put on—there's a dressing-gown of mine in the bathroom.' He jerked his thumb towards a panelled door in the corner of the saloon. 'Once you're decent, you can come back in here—and then we'll play the game by my rules.'

Without waiting to argue, she rolled off the sofa, landing in an undignified heap on the thick-piled carpet.

Picking herself up, tripping over the trailing corner of the blanket, she dived through the door he had indicated, closing and locking it behind her. And then she leaned back against it, sliding slowly to the floor, her eyes closed, her whole body shaking in reaction.

Anyone who knew her only as the cool, self-assured chief executive of the huge Geldard Corporation would have been hard-pressed to recognise her as this frightened, bedraggled creature, huddled on the floor, trembling and crying, trapped on a stranger's yacht—a stranger who had made his intentions absolutely clear.

But then she was the only one who knew how false was the façade she showed to the world. At twenty-seven years old, with never even the slightest hint of a romantic involvement, it was inevitable, perhaps, that certain myths had grown up around her—indeed, she had deliberately cultivated them as part of her defence. Her eyes could freeze impertinence at twenty paces— few saw the hint of vulnerability in the softness of her delicately drawn mouth.

As sole heir to her grandfather's substantial fortune, she had always known that any man who showed an interest in her was only trying to get his hands on her money or control of the Geldard empire. And she had learned to recognise the shallow compliments on her looks for what they were. Her blonde colouring and fine skin were well enough, and she would acknowledge that she had a good figure, kept in trim by regular exercise, but the Geldard features which had given her grandfather such an imposing air were really rather too strong for feminine beauty; a firm chin and a faintly patrician nose hinted at an assertiveness that terrified most men of her acquaintance.

And that was the way she liked it. She had never cared to put Grandfather's teaching to the test—she had her own mother's example as a constant reminder of the consequences of falling in love. Not that she, Georgia, would ever do anything as foolish as running off with a driving instructor—the ease with which the young man had been willing to be bought off had shown him up in his true colours.

She had grown up with the story of how Grandfather had brought home the jilted bride, chastened—and pregnant. Regrettably, her mother had further disappointed him by producing a mere girl instead of the longed-for grandson to inherit the biscuits-to-brewery empire he was busy building, and her weakness of character had further revealed itself in a steadily worsening drink problem. Georgia remembered her only as a pale wraith, haunting the overheated orangery at the back of the house, her breath always smelling of sherry, terrifying her with tearful attempts to make her sit on her lap. She had died almost unnoticed when Georgia was ten.

Surprisingly, however, Grandfather had taken to his granddaughter from the time she could toddle, and she had grown up to be the apple of his eye. She had inherited his biting intelligence and determination, and he had groomed her to take over the reins of the company as if she had been a boy.

And she had accepted that the privileges she enjoyed had their price, never allowing herself to regret that her wealth set her apart from the romantic pleasures of other young women of her age. Strictly trained to despise the weakness that had destroyed her mother, she was happy with her solitary state—most of the time; it was only sometimes at night, waking from a fitful dream with an aching sense of unfulfilled need, that she would even admit to herself that she was lonely...

But Grandfather would never have approved of her sitting here feeling sorry for herself, she reminded herself crisply—and she hadn't escaped from César's clutches only to fall victim to the notorious Jake Morgan! Pulling herself together with an effort of will, she sat up and looked around, taking careful stock of her surroundings.

It had grown dark outside, and sliding to her feet she found the switch that turned on the lights. The soft glow of silk-shaded lamps filled the room, gleaming on the rich, dark mahogany walls. This must be the master state-room—spacious and elegant, it had the same air of being an exclusively male province as the saloon. It was dominated by a huge bed, elevated on a low, carpeted platform and covered with wine-red silk sheets. What had she got herself into?

Curiosity drew her to explore, opening the doors set into the wood-panelled walls. One revealed a cavernous fitted wardrobe, half-empty—just a couple of beautifully-tailored business suits and hand-made silk shirts, but mostly good quality casual clothes, several pairs of rugged denim jeans and a stack of different coloured T-shirts. Another revealed a small television set and a large hi-fi, and a column of CDs which told her nothing but that his taste in music ran from jazz to hard rock, with a little country and a few unexpected classics thrown in.

The last door opened to reveal a bathroom of hedon-istic black marble, complete with a huge, deep sunken bath with gold taps that would have been at home in a Roman potentate's palace. And gazing back at her from the mirrored wall opposite was her own reflection. She stared at it, strangely disturbed to see herself standing there in such an alien environment, her eyes glittering darkly and her mouth as soft as bruised raspberries, the blanket slipping from her naked shoulders...

'We'll play the game by my rules...' It didn't take much imagination to guess what he meant by that, she mused, stealing an apprehensive glance back at that big bed. Suddenly a vivid image rose in her mind, of her own creamy-gold skin against those wine-red sheets—overlaid with a deeply-bronzed, hard-muscled body...

Quickly she shook her head, alarmed by the rapid acceleration of her heartbeat. She had wasted too much time already—at any minute he might grow impatient, and come in to see why she was taking so long. Stepping over to the window, she uttered a sigh of relief; her luck was holding—from the moonlit contours of the coastline she knew that they were sailing into Mangrove Bay, the exclusive hide-away where her own yacht was moored. It was really no coincidence, of course—naturally Jake Morgan would choose to stay at the best place on the island.

Seeking and finding the window that doubled as emergency exit, she pushed it open. She had nothing on beneath the blanket, but she couldn't do anything about that now. Anyway, it was dark—with luck, she could get back on board her own yacht without anyone seeing her. Dropping the damp blanket to the floor, she clambered out of the window.

She couldn't avoid making a splash as she tumbled into the water, but hopefully all the attention of the crew would be on the task of manoeuvring the big boat into a suitable anchoring spot among the others dotted around the bay. Striking swiftly away from the hull, she swam underwater for a short distance as an added precaution, before surfacing and looking around to get her bearings.

It took her only a moment to identify the *Geldard Star*. All appeared quiet on board—her captain would have waited, consulted with the company's lawyers before raising a full-scale alarm. The swim-steps were down and she crept up them, keeping low.

Jake Morgan's boat was no more than two or three hundred yards away, dropping anchor and tying up to a mooring-bouy with all the usual commotion and to-ing and fro-ing of crew—enough to distract the attention of her own look-outs for a crucial moment or two. Like a ghost she slipped across the deck and into the darkened saloon, at last reaching the safety of her own elegant state-room. Closing the door behind her, she leaned against it, sighing with relief.

There had been moments, during the past couple of hours, when she had thought she was in serious trouble. But her grandfather had taught her never to give in, to keep planning her moves—the winners were the ones who really *believed* they could win, he always said. And she had won; she was back on her own ground, she could get some clothes on and stroll back out on deck, and unless she gave permission no one would even dare question where she had been. It would be as if none of it had happened.

The *Geldard Star* was one of the biggest boats in the bay, but Jake Morgan's boat was even bigger; from her cabin she could see straight across to it. A solitary figure stood on the fore-deck, looking out over the dark waters of the sound towards the open channel between Spanish Point and Maria Hill—as if looking for mermaids.

A small shiver of heat ran down her spine as she remembered those glittering dark eyes, sweeping down over her naked body with such mocking contempt. No, it couldn't *quite* be as if those past few hours had never happened, she reflected uneasily; she wasn't going to be able to forget those kisses.

Absently she touched her fingertips to her lips, feeling still the warm softness that had melted them so sweetly. No, she wasn't going to be able to forget.

CHAPTER TWO

THE office of the chief executive of the Geldard Corporation was on the top floor of Geldard House, one of the tallest blocks in the City, with a spectacular view over London—from the silver ribbon of the Thames almost at its feet to the distant blue-grey hills of Hertfordshire, away beyond its northern suburbs.

Georgia could vividly recall the first time she had come up here with her grandfather, when the building had still been a concrete shell. Stomping around in his yellow hard-hat, doling out orders right and left to the builders, he had insisted on walking almost to the edge of the open floor—the point where she was standing now—though then there had been no glass in place and the wind had been whistling through like a hurricane.

But old George Geldard had cared for nothing, not even the forces of nature—and certainly not for the fact that the costs of the building were spiralling while the prospects of letting space in it were tumbling. 'Hold your nerve,' he had used to say whenever she'd queried the wisdom of it. 'Keep planning your moves. If you believe you can win, you *will* win.'

He had lived just long enough to see it completed— the pinnacle of his empire and very nearly its ruin. To finance it he had been forced to float a new share issue, even though it had meant losing overall control of the company; he had planned it to be only a short-term measure, until he could afford to buy back enough shares to hold a majority once again. She had been working to achieve that ever since.

The task would have been easier if it hadn't been for the constant, bitter rivalry between her two uncles; it was ironic that in his disappointment at her birth her grandfather had settled blocks of shares on his own nephew and his wife's, believing the management of the company would one day have to pass into their hands— they were so busy fighting each other, they couldn't have managed a prayer meeting in a nunnery.

It had largely been their inability to agree on a compromise candidate that had enabled her to win the boardroom battle to be elected chief executive—in spite of the Old Man's wishes, it had been no foregone conclusion. And in the three years since then she had had to fight every inch of the way to prove to the sceptics— particularly within the more conservative institutional holdings—that she was neither too young, nor the wrong gender, to shoulder such a substantial responsibility.

She knew that there were many who were watching and waiting for her to make a mistake. But she had worked damned hard, and at last she was beginning to feel that she was respected in her own right, not just as the Old Man's granddaughter. It amused her when she heard herself described as a chip off the old block— even—the highest accolade—as George Geldard the Second.

Of course, the price of her success had been high—a single-minded ambition that could permit nothing to distract her. But it was a price she had always been willing to pay; she had every reason to be happy with her life— she had everything that money could buy. It would just be greedy to ask for anything more...

A discreet tap at the door brought her out of her reverie, and she moved back to her desk. 'Come in.'

'Georgia? Sorry to interrupt—I hope you weren't busy?'

Bernard Harrison had been the company secretary for almost fifteen years; loyal and dependable, he was one of the few people she felt she could trust. She smiled at him warmly. 'Not at all,' she assured him. 'I was just day-dreaming, I'm afraid.'

He frowned, studying her in some concern. 'That's not like you. But you do look tired, you know—you ought to take a holiday.'

'I had a holiday in February,' she reminded him with a touch of asperity.

'Yes—but that was almost three months ago,' he countered, with the bluntness of one who could remind her what she had looked like in a gym-slip, with her hair in bunches. 'And, to be honest, it didn't look as if it did you a great deal of good. I know you don't want to tell me what happened that last afternoon—'

'Nothing happened,' she returned with uncharacteristic impatience. 'Heavens, I was only gone for a couple of hours—anyone would think I'd been missing for a week! I just went for a walk, that's all.'

'Without telling anyone where you were going...'

'So I was irresponsible for one afternoon! Good heavens, I was on holiday—I felt like being off the leash for a while, just being like any other holidaymaker, strolling around without anyone knowing who I was... Anyway, what was it you wanted, Bernard?' she added, quickly changing the subject before he could probe any more.

'You asked me to try to find out a little about this holding company that's been buying up our shares,' he reminded her, laying a slim file on the desk; the label, neatly printed in his own square hand, proclaimed ''Falcon Holdings''. 'Not much success, I'm afraid— it's owned by a company in New York, which in turn is owned by a private trust registered in the Bahamas.'

Georgia sighed, picking up the file. 'I was afraid of that,' she mused wryly. 'I suppose there's no way of finding out who controls the trust?'

Bernard shook his head. 'I've tried, but it's like banging your head against a brick wall when you come up against their rules of banking secrecy.'

'Ah, well . . . Thank you, Bernard—you did your best. We'll just have to watch things very carefully. If there *is* a bid, do you think we'll be able to fight it off?'

'I would hope so,' he assured her soberly. 'I think we'd be able to keep most of the private shareholders with us. It's the institutions I'd be concerned about—if the offer was high enough, they'd have to think very seriously about their own sharedholders' interests.'

Georgia clenched her fist. 'I'll fight it, Bernard,' she declared. 'Every inch—they'll find I won't be a walkover.'

'No one would expect anything else from you—the way you've run this company for the past three years proves that. Incidentally,' he added on a note of diffidence, 'this may be no more than a coincidence—but on the other hand . . . ?'

He put a copy of one of the more sensationalist tabloid newspapers down on the desk in front of her. She glanced up at him in amused surprise, and then her heart gave a sudden thud as she recognised the man in the front-page picture beneath the blazoned headline, LUCKY DIGGER.

Only the iron self-control instilled by her grandfather enabled her to conceal her reaction.

Australian business tycoon Jake Morgan arrived in Britain last week, and already he's got two new women in his life—stunning dark-haired supermodel girl-friend Sheena Smith, and winning three-year-old racehorse Blondie . . .

Blondie...?

Even in the black and white newsprint there was an unmistakable air of arrogance in the set of those wide shoulders, a challenging glint in those deep-set eyes. He'd been here a week, the story said—but it didn't say why he'd come or how long he was planning to stay. She picked up the Falcon Holdings file in her other hand, eyeing it speculatively.

'Yes, you...could be right, Bernard,' she managed, somehow keeping her voice steady. 'Well spotted.'

Had he found out who she was? It had probably been inevitable—though unlike him she sought to avoid personal publicity as much as possible. Newspaper editors seemed to be fascinated by the fact that a female—particulary a young blonde female—was running such a substantial company, and couldn't resist using a photograph of her whenever they ran a story about Geldard's. But she had hoped that he might not recognise her—after all, she had been soaking wet at the time they had met.

Well, if he thought he would be able to use that incident to blackmail her in some way, he would be disappointed, she vowed resolutely. No one knew about it, and she would simply deny that it had ever happened.

The May Day Ball in aid of the Geldard Foundation was one of the most glittering events of the social calendar. The foundation had been another of her grandfather's grand gestures, set up to support research into heart disease—unfortunately he had stubbornly refused to listen himself to the advice available, dismissing all his doctor's pleas to give up his brandy and cigars.

The grand ballroom of one of London's top hotels was the venue for the occasion, where two hundred and fifty of the cream of society could dine and dance in elegant style into the small hours of the morning while being parted from as much money as possible in the name of a good cause.

Georgia cast a last anxious glance over the setting as the first of the Bentleys and Rolls Royces began to disgorge their elegant occupants outside the imposing entrance. It was as near perfect as six long months of hard work by the committee—and several days by the staff of the hotel—could make it. Long white-clothed tables, awash with silver and crystal, sparkled beneath the massive chandeliers that swung from the lofty ceiling, and the wide expanse of parquet dance-floor gleamed with polish.

It had occurred to her more than once that it would probably be a great deal easier to call the whole thing off and simply write to people asking for a financial contribution, instead of going to these lengths to prise open their wallets. But she was aware that her grandfather had had a more cynical motive in mind—it did the company a great deal of good commercially to be associated with such a prestigious social event.

'Georgie, darling! What a fabulous dress! And the Geldard diamonds too, I see. So *that's* the reason why some of these "waiters" have such magnificent shoulders!'

Georgia turned, smiling in welcome for her old schoolfriend, now married into the minor echelons of the aristocracy. 'I'm afraid so,' she responded lightly. 'The insurance company insisted on it. I'd really rather leave the damned things in the vault and wear paste.'

'Oh no, surely not,' Margot protested, shocked. 'They're so beautiful—if they were mine, I'd wear them all the time. Even to bed! Especially if one of those gorgeous hunks had to come along to keep an eye on them!' she added outrageously, slanting a flirtatious eye over one of the stone-faced security-guards who had been assigned to protect the priceless gems around Georgia's

throat, his bulk not too discreetly concealed beneath the
white dinner jacket of a waiter.

Georgia shook her head, laughing. 'Margot, you're
impossible! You're supposed to be a respectable married
woman these days.'

'Me? Respectable?' her friend gurgled. 'Not likely. Oh,
Charles is a dear, but he's just a *husband*, after all. But
what about you?' she added, frowning slightly as she
held Georgia at arm's length and subjected her to a
critical survey. 'How *do* you keep your figure? I'll swear
you're even slimmer than the last time I saw you, and
yet you eat like a horse!'

'Oh, I...get a lot of exercise,' Georgia explained,
waving one beautifully manicured hand in a dismissive
gesture. 'And I...had a slight bout of flu or something
earlier this year.'

'Flu, huh?' Margot's searching eyes were watching her
face for the slightest betraying flicker. 'Not a man, then?'

'Of course not!' Georgia concealed a stab of alarm at
her friend's shrewd guess. 'Why on earth should you
think that?'

'It's usually the only way I ever get to lose any weight,'
Margot confessed ruefully. 'Excitement while I'm falling
in love, and pining when it's all over! Though now I'm
married I suppose I shall have to forego all that sort of
fun.'

'It doesn't sound much like fun to me,' Georgia returned drily.

Margot chuckled. 'Ah, you ought to try it. In fact,
it's about time you did—it would do you good. Your
grandfather's got a lot to answer for, you know—I
suppose he was only trying to do what he thought was
best for you, but he ended up convincing you that no
man could be interested in you for any other reason than
your money.'

'Don't be ridiculous, Margot,' Georgia protested, aware of a slight waver in her voice. 'Oh, you'll have to excuse me—I see some more guests arriving. I'd better go and do my duty.' And she slipped away before her friend could ask any more probing questions.

As she crossed the foyer she caught a fleeting glimpse of her own reflection in the large gilded mirror on the wall. Was Margot right? Had her grandfather made her too suspicious? The image that looked back at her seemed to mock her. Poor little rich girl, it seemed to say—you've got everything, and yet you've got nothing.

Her hairdresser had swept up her hair in an elegant style, and her slim-fitting dress of silver-white satin had a pure simplicity of line, cut low across the honey-smooth curve of her breasts, hugging her slender figure right down to her ankles—all the better to show off the fabulous Geldard diamonds.

She didn't actually like them very much; they were rather too ostentatious for her taste—a heavy collar of sparkling white gems, set in gold, with matching drops swinging from her small ears. They were reputed to be part of the Russian Crown Jewels, though Georgia was inclined to doubt the truth of that. Her grandfather had bought them for her grandmother as a silver wedding present; that lady, a plain Yorkshirewoman, had thought it a terrible waste of money, and Georgia heartily agreed with her—most of the time they were locked up in the vaults at the bank.

But at least while she wore them no one would doubt that the Geldard fortune was as healthy as ever. And if she was going to have to fight a hostile takeover bid, it was vital to keep up appearances.

'Great party, Georgie! Just about everyone's here!'

Georgia smiled, discreetly weaving her partner out of a potential collision; Robin Rustrom-Smith was an excellent dancer when he was sober, but at the moment he wasn't. 'Yes, it's going very well,' she agreed, glancing around the crowded room with satisfaction.

"Everyone" was indeed there—aristocrats rubbing shoulders with film stars and captains of industry, all willing to abandon their dignity to compete fiercely in a game of bingo to win trinkets that had cost less than they'd spend on breakfast, or to scrabble for the prize balloons. A swift glance at the slim Cartier watch on her wrist told her that it was almost midnight; she could at last begin to relax in the knowledge that the ball had raised a great deal of money for the foundation...

Suddenly she stiffened as a tall figure near the door caught her eye. It wasn't the first time this had happened—several times over the past three months she had spotted a man of a certain height and build, with dark blond hair curling over his collar at the back, and her heart had tripped over itself until inevitably a second look confirmed that it was a complete stranger.

But this time she didn't need a second look; there was no mistaking the arrogant set of those wide shoulders, the tilt of his head as he surveyed the room. The formal dinner jacket he was wearing was beautifully cut, but the vivid memory that flashed into her mind was of his bare chest, hard-muscled and bronzed by the sun, scattered with rough, curling, male hair...

Her heart fluttering in panic, she nudged Robin across to the far side of the dance-floor—fortunately his brain was rather too fuddled by the excellent champagne that had been flowing generously all evening for him to notice anything amiss. Hidden by the crowd of dancers, she watched warily, like a small mouse hiding in the long grass, hoping the farmyard cat wouldn't notice she was there.

She had known that there was a risk that she would run into him if he stayed in England for any length of time. But what was he doing here tonight? His name wasn't on the guest-list; and besides, he had only just arrived—if he had been there at dinner, she would certainly have seen him. Was it just an unlucky chance, or had he come looking for her?

Waltzing around the crowded dance-floor, she was barely aware of the music or of the glittering gathering enjoying themselves with an increasing degree of boisterousness beneath the sparkling chandeliers high above their heads, pastel-coloured balloons drifting around their feet, curling lengths of streamer decorating their hair and shoulders.

As the dance came to an end she was surrounded at once by a throng of admirers, clamouring for the chance of being next to lead her round the floor.

'My turn, Georgie.'

'Georgie, you promised me.'

'Pardon the intrusion from the far-flung Colonies, boys, but I think this is my dance.'

It was that lazy, mocking drawl she had tried so hard to forget. To Georgia's disgust, not one of the other claimants to her hand seemed willing to challenge the newcomer; groaning in protest, they conceded defeat, standing aside to let him step in. He held out one imperious hand, and she could do nothing but put hers in it and let him draw her out onto the dance-floor and into his arms.

He danced well, for a man who looked as if he'd be more at home on horseback, herding half a million sheep across the outback, she reflected with a touch of asperity. And she couldn't deny that the elegant cut of a formal dinner jacket suited him remarkably well. But the memory of the last time he had held her in his arms was swirling in her brain, and all her usual cool poise had deserted her, leaving her feeling as gauche as a schoolgirl.

His soft laughter mocked her. 'Well, good evening, Blondie. This *is* a pleasant surprise.'

She lifted her eyes to stare up at him. 'What are you doing here?' she demanded raggedly.

'I bribed my way in,' he admitted without shame. 'I'm staying here at the hotel, and I was passing across the hall when I happened to look in—and who should I see but my little mermaid? So I collared one of those fearsome old dragons who always seem to run these things, and gave her a nice fat cheque to let me in. I was hoping I might run into you while I was in London, but I certainly didn't expect it to be here.' His voice took on a note of sardonic amusement. 'I almost didn't recognise you... with your clothes on.'

She returned him a look of cool dignity which she hoped would override the betraying hint of pink in her cheeks. 'If you're going to make coarse remarks like that, I shall walk off the dance-floor.'

He chuckled with laughter, the arm around her waist tightening just a fraction, as if to warn her not to try it. 'I see you got your diamonds,' he remarked, a hard edge in his voice. 'Quite a set—the real thing too. You *have* been busy since the last time we met. Found yourself some rich fool to marry, did you? Who is it? That pasty-faced creep you were dancing with when I came in?'

'Robin isn't a creep!' she protested hotly.

'He isn't man enough for you.' He had drawn her closer, his warm breath stirring her hair, his hand sliding slowly down the length of her spine to mould intimately over the smooth curve of her derrière. 'Don't you sometimes wish, when you feel his scrawny hands on your smooth, satin skin, for a *real* lover?' he taunted provocatively. 'One whose touch would be warm and gentle on your soft, naked body—who would caress those ripe, firm, beautiful breasts with tenderness and who would make love to you all night, in every way you could possibly imagine...?'

Georgia drew in a sharp breath, shocked not so much by his words as by her own reaction to them; breathing the musky, male scent of him was conjuring a memory of that brief encounter on his yacht, a memory so vivid that she felt as if she was once again naked in his arms, her mouth bruised by his kisses, her creamy smooth skin flushed beneath that insolent dark gaze.

It took a considerable effort of will to regather the scattered threads of her composure. But she couldn't let herself weaken—she knew only too well how swiftly he could take advantage of any lowering of her resistance. From beneath her lashes, she studied him warily. It seemed that he still didn't know who she was. It was possible, of course—he had been here no more than a few minutes, and he might not have bothered to ask anyone her name.

Or, on the other hand, he could be playing some kind of cruel game with her. If he *was* the mysterious figure behind the holding company that was buying up Geldard shares, she was quite sure he would try to use their previous meeting to gain an unfair advantage—there was no mistaking the hint of ruthlessness about that hard mouth.

Either way, she had to keep her nerve, keep planning her moves. And, for the moment, it seemed that the best tactic was to play the confident, sexually assured siren he had taken her for. It was hardly a role that came naturally to her, but all she had to do was copy Margot's style—it couldn't be that difficult.

Slanting him a flirtatious smile, she lifted her eyes to his. 'I...didn't know you were planning to come to England,' she remarked carefully. 'You didn't mention it.'

Only the slightest flicker of those dark eyes registered his surprise at her change of manner. 'Well, now, as I recall we didn't get too much time to talk about anything before you disappeared from my life,' he responded on a note of mocking humour. 'But since the only thing I knew about you was that you were English—at least I figured that from your accent—it seemed like the best way to find you was to come to London.'

Heavens, he must think she was stupid! She laughed lightly, hiding her annoyance behind a gloss of sophisticated amusement. 'Really? You didn't exactly rush, though—it's been nearly three months.'

'Ah, well... Unfortunately there were one or two business matters that forced me to go back to Australia first,' he explained. 'But I came as soon as I could.'

She shook her head, mimicking Margot's best arch mannerisms. 'No, really—what are you doing here?' she persisted. 'Do you have business interests in England?'

'A few,' he conceded, those enigmatic dark eyes giving nothing away. 'I'm just looking around for anything that catches my eye. I've already picked up a nice little filly—as a matter of fact I named her Blondie, after you.'

Georgia's jaw was aching with the effort of maintaining her smile. 'So I saw in the paper. Am I supposed to be flattered?'

'I like the name,' he countered genially. 'And I don't know your real one.'

She laughed the implied question aside. 'And where's your other ''filly'' tonight?' she enquired, trying for an air of worldly unconcern. 'Not with you?'

'You mean Sheena? No, she's working—Paris or Rome or somewhere. Why do you ask?'

'Oh, just... mildly curious,' she responded, not quite able to keep her voice as even as she would have liked.

'Not jealous, by any chance, are you?' he taunted.

'Jealous? Of course not.' She shrugged her slim shoulders in a gesture of unconcern. 'I have no reason to be jealous.'

'No, you don't,' he murmured, drawing her closer again. 'She's *almost* as beautiful as you, but she doesn't kiss like you. You tasted like honey and melted in my arms like a dream...'

'I was... half-drowned,' she choked out, her mask abruptly slipping.

'So you were,' he conceded softly, mockingly. 'But you're not half-drowned now.'

With a small stab of alarm she realised that he had waltzed her out through the open French windows at the far end of the dance-floor into a cool marble atrium, where a green cast-iron fountain played amid a riot of tropical palms beneath a high glass-domed ceiling. Before she could protest, he had drawn her back into the shadows behind one of the Doric columns that ran around the outer rim, and his mouth had claimed hers in a kiss that she didn't know how to resist.

His lips moved over hers, warm and sensuous, and with a soft sigh she surrendered to their sweet persuasion, granting him admission to the moist, secret depths he sought. The musky male scent of his skin was drugging her mind, stirring an instinctive response that was far beyond the reach of reason.

She was curving herself into his demanding embrace, her tender breasts crushed against the hard wall of his chest, her spine melting in the heat that was swirling in her blood. His sensuous tongue coiled around hers as his hands moulded intimately over the soft curves of her body with that warm, tender touch he had promised...

'Why did you disappear like that?' he breathed, the husky timbre of his voice caressing her. 'I thought I'd never see you again. If it hadn't been for one very damp blanket on the floor by the open window I might have thought you were a figment of my dreams. And now that I've found you, I don't want to let you go—I want to make love to you...'

Abruptly his words brought her back to reality. What in hell was she doing, letting him kiss her again when she knew that he was a threat to everything she had worked for—everything her grandfather had worked for? Summoning all her strength, she forced her hands between them, struggling to push him away.

'Damn that bloodless creep and his diamonds,' he cursed, misunderstanding her reaction. 'I can buy you diamonds—all the diamonds you want. Come upstairs to my suite and let me remind you what it's like to be touched by hands that still have some warmth in them...'

'Stop it—let me go...' she begged, her voice rising in panic. 'Leave me alone...'

'It's all right, Miss Geldard, we've got him!'

As Georgia blinked in bewilderment a sixteen-stone gorilla in a white dinner jacket caught Jake from behind in a massive bear-hug, dragging him off her as another swung a punch at his head. With the instincts of a street-fighter he ducked, the blow hitting the first gorilla square on the jaw as Jake barged the second in a low rugby tackle, bringing him down in a sprawling heap—and the world erupted in a mêlée of flying fists and the exploding flashbulbs of Press cameras.

'Stop it! You've made a mistake!' she cried, wishing she could vanish through the floor as the atrium filled with curious guests, coming out to stare.

Slowly the struggling mass on the floor resolved itself into three bruised and bloodied men, who drew cautiously apart and rose to their feet, eyeing each other with considerable hostility and suspicion. Jake shook his head, pulling a handkerchief from his pocket to dab gingerly at a trickle of blood on his lip.

'Would somebody mind telling me what in hell's going on?' he demanded, looking from his assailants to Georgia and back again.

She drew in a deep, steadying breath. 'I'm . . . sorry,' she managed, conscious of the flaming heat in her cheeks. 'These men are from the security firm responsible for protecting my diamonds.'

'We thought you was trying to pinch 'em,' the first gorilla supplied. 'I'm sorry, Miss Geldard—we was watching you dancing and everything looked kosher. Then the next minute you was missing, and when we got out here it looked like you was . . . having a bit of bother. I . . . suppose we jumped to the wrong conclusion,' he added sheepishly. 'No hard feelings, mate?' he added to Jake. 'We was just doing our job.'

Jake grinned, accepting the massive hand that was being held out to him. 'No hard feelings,' he conceded, the glint of amusement in his half-closed eye suggesting to Georgia that he had quite enjoyed the scrap.

'You put up a damned good show,' the other gorilla admitted with wry admiration. 'If you're ever looking for a job, we could use you on the firm.'

'Thank you,' Jake responded, shaking his hand solemnly. 'I hope I won't ever need to be, but if I am I'll remember that.'

The flashbulbs exploded again, to catch the moment. 'Miss Geldard, what are the diamonds worth?' one of the photographers called out, delighted with this unexpected bonus on an evening when they had anticipated nothing more than deadly dull society snaps.

With a swift step, Jake interposed himself between her and the cameras. 'I think you have enough pictures,' he asserted grimly. 'Miss Geldard is tired.'

There was a murmur of protest, but no one seemed inclined to argue with him. With some reluctance, the crowd and the photographers drifted slowly back to the ballroom. The security guards were the last to go, leaving them alone.

Georgia lifted her hand to her hair, trying in vain to tuck back the strands that were slipping from the elegant arrangement her hairdresser had created. Nervously she flicked a glance up at Jake, who was leaning one wide shoulder against the stone pillar beside them, easing his grazed knuckles.

'Well, *Miss Geldard*,' he remarked, adding a sardonic emphasis to her name. 'I suppose you could say that we've now been formally introduced—in a manner of speaking.'

She lowered her lashes, her cheeks flushing faintly pink. 'Yes, well... I'm very sorry for the... misunderstanding...'

He shouted with laughter. 'Well, that's an understatement! There was I, thinking you'd found yourself a nice wealthy sugar-daddy, and what do you know? Turns out you're a little Croesus in your own right!' He lifted the heavy diamond collar around her throat on one finger, regarding it with the expert eye of one who knew his gem-stones. 'Very nice too—and worth a cool half a million, at least. No wonder you need bodyguards.'

'Quite.' With an effort of will, she lifted her eyes to meet his, all her icy dignity restored. 'However, although there's no "bloodless creep" on the scene, I'm afraid I must regretfully decline your charming invitation to go upstairs to your suite. I have no taste for casual one-night stands.'

He laughed without humour. 'That wasn't exactly what I had in mind.'

'Oh? And what *did* you have in mind?'

He regarded her for a moment in quizzical assessment, and then he shook his head. 'No, I don't think this is quite the right moment to explain,' he responded. 'Why didn't you tell me who you were?'

She hesitated, drawing in a long, steadying breath. 'I don't think this is quite the right moment to explain,' she countered crisply. 'I'm sorry about the misunderstanding with the security people—I hope your injuries aren't serious?'

'I'll live,' he returned, an inflection of sardonic humour in his voice as he cautiously felt his swollen eye. 'Ow! Those guys can sure pack a wallop!'

'I'll ask the kitchen to send you up a raw steak.'

'You could try kissing it better. . .' he taunted, leaning his hands against the wall on each side of her shoulders to trap her between his arms.

Her blue eyes flashed him a frost warning, and she ducked neatly under his arm. 'I'll ask the kitchen to send you up a raw steak,' she reiterated dampeningly as she turned him an aloof shoulder and walked back to the ballroom.

He chuckled with wry amusement. 'You know, you should always wear diamonds,' he remarked in lazy mockery. 'They go with your eyes.'

CHAPTER THREE

'DECENT shiner you've got there, old man.'

Jake squinted out of his good eye, smiling wryly as the pale young man, whom he recognised as the one he had mistaken for Georgia's rich sugar-daddy, came over to join him, leaning against the bonnet of the Range Rover. 'You should see the other guy.'

Robin Rustrom-Smith chuckled. 'I had a ringside seat. It's all over the papers, you know. Our Sweet Georgia is not going to be best pleased with you—doesn't like that sort of publicity.'

Jake shrugged his wide shoulders in a dismissive gesture, holding his binoculars gingerly to his eyes to watch the string of horses galloping across the soft Lambourn turf. 'How was I supposed to know who she was? She never told me her name.'

'Ah, so that's why you were so reckless. You got off lightly, you know—the last chap who tried it on with her still bears the scars.'

'You don't say,' Jake drawled with laconic humour.

'No, I'm serious. Took her horsewhip to him—lovely aim, straight across the cheek. Ten years ago, that was—no one else has dared risk it once.'

Jake lowered his binoculars, turning to stare at his genial informant in frank astonishment. 'You mean...no one?' he queried. 'No one's even...? But she'd have been...what, sixteen?'

'Seventeen.'

'Oh, come on!' Jake laughed. 'You're kidding me. A

good-looking broad like that? She must have 'em queuing in the aisles!'

Robin shook his head. 'If there'd been any action, I'd have known about it—m'sister Margot's one of her best friends, and you know what women are for talking about that sort of thing. Oh, I agree she's a great girl, but when it comes to trying it on with her... To tell you the truth, even the thought of it scares me into the middle of next week—and I've known her since we were children.'

'So you mean she's still...?'

Robin nodded in cheerful confirmation. 'Of course, it was the Old Man's fault—her grandfather. The tight-fisted old goat was always convinced that anyone who looked twice at her was after his money, so he all but locked her up in a chastity belt and threw away the key. Siberia, we used to call her at school—couldn't warm her up with a blowtorch.'

'Well, well...' Jake lifted his binoculars again. 'Well, well, well...' That was certainly no longer true—as he had every reason to know. Or was that the sort of game she played? He had met the kind before, promising everything and then refusing to deliver until they had got whatever it was they wanted—usually a ring on their finger and a meal-ticket for life.

Not that the frostbitten Miss Geldard had any need of a meal ticket—she could afford to buy not only her own lunch, but the whole damned restaurant if she chose. Nor did she need to resort to those sort of tactics to get herself a husband, if that was what she wanted—with one snap of her fingers she could have half the available men this side of the Rockies queuing up for her hand.

So what was it? Some kind of power trip? Was that what turned her on? Didn't she have enough power as chief executive of her family firm? But then he had met a lot of *men* to whom power was like a drug—the more of it they had, the more they needed. Why shouldn't some women be like that? And in her position she must have to fight her way in a man's world every day of her working life—what better way to even the score than by hitting back below the belt, as it were . . . ?

Damn, he never had been able to resist a challenge—especially one with such a prize at the end of it! The thought of teaching Miss Geldard the danger of playing power games with the big boys, and at the same time disproving his new acquaintance's blowtorch theory, was tempting enough to make his mouth water. Ice would never have melted more sweetly into honey . . . !

A third off-roader pulled up in the field, the driver climbing out and strolling over to join them, calling a casual greeting. Jake vaguely recalled having met him before—and not liking him much. He had wondered then what had caused the faint white scar down his right cheek.

'Nice looking filly you've got there,' the newcomer remarked, studying the horses in training through his own binoculars. 'I was after her myself.'

'Were you?' Jake smiled grimly, the amusing irony of the remark not lost on him.

Robin chuckled softly to himself. 'You'd best be careful, Nige,' he put in, with the air of one feeding fuel to a fire. 'Looks like he's making a habit of picking up fillies you were interested in.'

The Honourable Nigel Woodvine cast his old school-friend a withering look down his aristocratic nose.

'I've just been telling him about our Georgie,' Robin supplied. 'He doesn't seem to believe me.'

Nigel turned his cool survey on Jake, letting his lip curl into a slight sneer. 'Is that so?' he queried, carefully calculating a degree of disdain that would fall just short of provoking any serious danger from those hard fists—he too had been present at the Geldard Foundation May

Day Ball. 'You think you can do better than the rest of us, then?'

Jake shrugged, returning the contempt. 'Could be.'

Nigel laughed unpleasantly. 'I doubt it. From what I gather, you've barely made it to first base. Granted, that's a little further than most people have got to with the damned frigid bitch—but you won't get her into bed.'

Jake examined his grazed hand, flexing the fingers contemplatively, wondering how the knuckles would stand up to another close encounter with hard bone. 'You don't reckon?' he mused, deceptively quiet.

Nigel lifted his binoculars, coolly watching the string of horses as they turned for home. 'No, I don't,' he confirmed. 'You putting that filly in for the Geldard Cup at Ascot in September?'

'I expect so.'

'I'll tell you what—I'll make a bet with you. My bay— the one leading the string there—against your filly says you can't get her into bed before the race.' He lowered his binoculars, his narrow eyes glinting. 'What do you say?'

Robin drew in a sharp breath. 'Hey, Nige...!' he protested, appalled. 'I mean, come on! You can't make a bet like that!'

'Can't I?' Again he gave that unpleasant laugh. 'Maybe our Australian friend doesn't think he can take up the challenge?'

Jake held his anger carefully in check; sometimes there were better ways of dealing with contemptible jerks like this over-bred Englishman than using your fists. Was he really considering accepting such a dumb bet? He'd never done anything like it in his life—even in his crass adolescence he wouldn't have dreamed of it. But maybe the stiff-necked Miss Geldard had it coming to her.

He lifted his own binoculars again, studying the elegant bay at the head of the string. 'A bit showy for my taste, but I wouldn't mind having her,' he drawled with mocking self-assurance. 'You're on.'

'Another red rose, Georgia.'

'Thank you, Janet. Throw it in the bin like the others, please.'

'Oh, but . . . It seems such a shame!' her secretary protested. 'He called three times yesterday, too.'

'If there's one thing I can't stand, it's a man who won't take no for an answer,' Georgia responded on a note of crisp dismissal. 'I'm leaving for my lunch appointment now, Janet. And if Mr Morgan rings again, the answer is still the same—no, I will not have lunch with him, nor dinner with him, nor will I go to the theatre or anywhere else with him.'

'Yes, Georgia,' Janet conceded with a wistful little sigh. Normally briskly efficient, there was a small, romantic corner in her soul that was highly susceptible to the rough-hewn charm of the big Australian who had been pursuing her hard-hearted boss with such determination for the past couple of weeks.

Georgia smiled grimly, and swung her handbag onto her shoulder. 'I have a meeting with Bernard at two-thirty, so I'll be back by two-fifteen. And I'll need the production figures for the Redford Road bakery by tonight—I have to write a briefing paper for next week's board meeting.'

Her secretary nodded, making a note. 'Do you want the figures for the past three years?'

'Better make it the past five. See you later, Janet.' She swept from the office, studiously ignoring the single, perfect red rose in its cellophane wrapper lying on Janet's desk. She had more than enough to worry about, without Jake Morgan pestering her. The mysterious Falcon Holdings was steadily buying up more of her shares; they had almost fifteen percent now—another fifteen and they would have to announce a formal bid. She had already decided to start discreetly liquidating some of her assets, ready to fight it.

And now, just when she didn't need it, she had been informed that one of the companies that owned a small but potentially important block of Geldard's shares had itself been taken over. Apparently it had been a friendly takeover, providing a rescue package that would save them from the hands of the receivers—which was fortunate for them. But it left her with a worrying question mark—would the new owners support her or not?

The executive lift took her down smoothly and swiftly to the basement, where her chauffeur was waiting with her ice-blue Rolls Royce to transport her to the restaurant where she was meeting a representative from the new owners of Linepaq to discuss their continuing association with Geldard's.

'Morning, Miss Geldard,' Maurice greeted her, opening the rear door.

'Good morning, Maurice. What's the traffic like?'

'Not too bad, miss. Shouldn't take us more than ten or fifteen minutes.'

'Thank you, Maurice.' She glanced at the slim gold watch on her wrist as she settled on the smooth Connolly hide rear seat and fastened her seat belt. She would be a little early; good—that suited her. She would have time to settle herself and be in control before her guest arrived.

As Maurice eased the car up the ramp and out into the May sunshine she glanced at the file on the seat beside her. She was meeting a Mr Watson, the financial director, probably a grey man, full of figures, she speculated wryly—what a waste of a sunny afternoon. Around the Tower of London the tourists were enjoying the early taste of summer, sitting on the grassy bank beneath the high white wall, licking melting ice-cream cones—and she had to have lunch with some boring accountant.

Laughing at herself, she shook her head. What was wrong with her lately? It wasn't like her to be discontented with her lot—she knew that she was very privileged. It was just... sometimes she envied people whose lives were a little simpler. But then they probably envied her, she reminded herself crisply—gliding by in her gleaming Rolls, bound for lunch at one of London's most exclusive eating-houses.

Le Périgourdin was a charming little restaurant, in a quiet street close to Covent Garden. By night it was a popular dining place for theatregoers, but by day it was also a favourite spot for business lunchers like herself. As Maurice dropped her at the door she reminded herself of another advantage of the privileges she enjoyed—she didn't have to face the impossible task of finding a parking space.

The head waiter knew her well, and came at once to greet her as she stepped through the door. The atmosphere was Provençal, with whitewashed walls, dark rustic beams and rush matting on the floor. At the back was a large white-walled conservatory, massed with ferns and ivies, opening onto a tiny patio where in summer the most favoured diners could always expect a seat.

It was there that Henri led her, settling her at a corner table with many compliments that made her laugh. 'Henri, you're impossible! You're making me blush.'

'But you look so beautiful when you blush,' he declared broadly.

'Henri, I have a very dull lunch with a very dull accountant, and I have to concentrate,' she pleaded.

'*Mai non*!' he protested. 'It is not right that so beautiful a lady should fill her mind always with business, business, business on such a lovely day! It is a day for strolling barefoot in the park, hand in hand with your lover, *n'est-ce pas*?'

She shook her head, still laughing—and then froze as a tall, familiar figure appeared in the doorway. He was casually dressed in close-fitting denim jeans and a white cotton shirt with the sleeves rolled back over strong, sun-bronzed forearms. The collar was unfastened at the throat and his loose blond hair was catching the sun; as he lounged towards her she felt her mouth go suddenly dry.

'Hello there, Blondie,' he greeted her lazily, hooking out a chair and sitting down.

Somehow she found her voice. 'Go away!' she protested, her eyes flashing angry sparks. 'I mean... I'm sorry, I'm meeting someone for lunch,' she amended, conscious of Henri hovering beside her, his broad smile dimmed with concern.

'I know,' Jake responded in that lazy, mocking drawl. 'Me.' He grinned up at the head waiter. 'We'll have the menu now, please. And I'll have a glass of lager, if you've got any. What'll you have to drink, Blondie?'

'Nothing!' she countered in a harsh undervoice. 'I'm not having lunch with you. And stop calling me Blondie.'

'She'll have lager too.'

'No, I won't! I don't drink beer.'

'I believe we have some excellent Australian lager in the refrigerator, sir,' Henri offered, recognising beneath that casual appearance a customer to be respected.

'Hey, that's great! Henri, isn't it? OK, two tubes of lager, Henri—frosted!'

Henri bowed himself away as if he had been asked for the finest Pinot Noir, leaving Georgia glaring at her companion over the table.

'How dare you?' she demanded. 'If you think I'm having lunch with you...!'

'But we have an appointment,' he reminded her, a provocative glint in those dark eyes. 'To discuss business.'

She drew in a sharp breath, struggling to control the racing beat of her heart. '*You've* taken over Linepaq?' she queried sharply.

'That's right,' he confirmed, leaning back lazily in his chair. 'We clinched the deal last week.'

'And this Mr Watson? Does he exist?' she enquired.

He shook his head. 'Made him up. It was a pretty expensive way to get you to have lunch with me, but it worked.'

Her mouth thinned into an angry line. 'If you expect me to believe that you took over a whole company just so you could have lunch with me...!'

'Well, maybe not *just* so I could have lunch with you,' he conceded. 'It gets me an automatic seat on your board, as well. So you won't be able to go on giving me the cold shoulder—you may as well just relax and enjoy it! Ah, well done, Henri.' He beamed as the head waiter himself reappeared with two tall ice-cold glasses of light beer on a silver tray.

'My pleasure, sir.' The portly Frenchman beamed back. 'The perfect thing for the thirst on such a warm day.'

'My sentiments entirely.' He took a long, cool draught of the lager. 'Ace!' he approved cheerfully.

'Thank you, sir. The waiter will bring the menu for you now.'

'Have you any idea how ridiculously out of place you look?' Georgia hissed across the table. 'This is a very smart restaurant—I'm surprised they even let you in, dressed like that! And drinking beer...!'

'It's good beer,' he responded. 'Besides, as Henri said, it's a very warm day—I think I'm the one most sensibly dressed. Why don't you take that jacket off?' he added, slanting a critical eye over her jade-green silk suit.

'Because... I'm not wearing anything underneath it,' she admitted, her cheeks scarlet.

He lifted one dark eyebrow in mocking speculation, his gaze lingering with insolent reminiscence over the soft swell of her breasts beneath the jade silk. 'Nothing at all?' he taunted softly. 'Not even a bra?'

'Well, of course a bra,' she amended, half choking. Her mouth felt dry, and without thinking she reached for her glass of lager, gulping it down nervously. 'We're...here to talk about business, not my underwear!' she insisted, not quite able to keep the tremor from her voice.

'Ah, but your underwear's so much more interesting to talk about,' he murmured, tipping his chair forward and leaning his arms on the table so that he was much closer to her. 'I love to see a woman in silk and lace. I'm not fussy about the colour...'

To her relief, the waiter arrived with the menus at that point, and in the distraction of selecting from the mouthwatering choice she was able to recover some semblance of composure. 'I'll have the Cassoulet d'Oleron,' she decided. 'Followed by...Côtelettes d'Agneau, with mange-tout and duchesse potatoes.'

'The same for me,' Jake added. 'And another couple of lagers.' As the waiter withdrew he regarded Georgia across the table, those deep-set hazel eyes glinting with wicked amusement. 'So,' he remarked, 'why have you been refusing to take my calls? I suppose you're expecting me to apologise for mistaking you for a gold-digger?'

'It...might help,' she acknowledged stiffly.

'Well, I'm not going to. Under the circumstances, I think it was quite an understandable mistake to make. I find a beautiful woman...'

'Beautiful?' she countered, arching one finely drawn eyebrow. 'Oh, please, spare me the fatuous compliments, at least—whatever else I am, I know I'm not beautiful.'

'I find a beautiful woman,' he reiterated, overriding her objection, 'drifting around in a silly little dinghy, stark naked...'

'I wasn't naked,' she protested, slanting a furtive glance at the people at the next table, hoping they couldn't hear their conversation. 'At least, not while I was in the dinghy. I had a bikini on—it...must have come off in the water.'

He accepted that amendment with a shrug. 'OK, but what the hell were you doing out there in the first place?' he queried. 'Surely you know how unpredictable the weather can be around there? A squall could have blown up at any time.'

'I...can't tell you why I was there,' she responded, her cheeks flushing faintly pink. 'Please don't raise the subject again.'

Those dark eyes glinted, mocking her retreat. 'All right—let's talk about something simple,' he conceded genially. 'This is supposed to be a business lunch, so let's talk business. Tell me about Geldard's.'

Georgia hesitated, eyeing him warily from beneath her lashes. She didn't trust him one inch, and the last thing she wanted was to have him on the board of Geldard's. But there didn't seem to be very much she could do about it; one of the terms of Linepaq's ownership of their shares was an automatic right to a seat on the board. Unless she could come up with a good sound reason why he should be disqualified, she would have to accept him.

At least the company was a nice, safe subject to talk about—and there wasn't much he couldn't find out with a little research anyway. So as they ate the excellent lunch she told him the history of Geldard's, right from its early days just after the war, when her grandfather, newly de-mobbed, had begun working in a small bakery in his home-town near Leeds and had later bought it from the owner—working up to eighteen hours a day, as he had loved to relate, baking the bread and delivering it himself from a horse-drawn cart before returning to open the shop for the day.

'He must have been quite a character,' Jake remarked. 'I'd have liked to have met him.'

'He was,' she responded with a wry smile. 'He always worked as hard as that—he never let up. The trouble was, he expected everyone else around him to do the same—and not many could take the pace. Also he hated having to delegate. Even when the company got so big, he still wanted to be in control of every detail—and he'd sack even his senior managers at the drop of a hat, sometimes just to keep the others on their toes. It was the biggest problem I had when I took over, persuading people that they really *could* work on their own initiative.'

Jake nodded. 'It's a big mistake to operate like that,' he agreed. 'But not uncommon among self-made men. They find it hard to believe that anyone else can ever be as good at the job as they can. So they stifle development—and because everything has to wait for their say-so there are constant delays and disruptions, which ultimately cost money.'

'Mmm . . .' She nodded meditatively; she had always found it difficult to be critical of her grandfather and his business methods, but there were still legacies of his autocratic rule that needed to be swept away.

'Were you fond of him?'

She glanced up at him in astonishment; 'fond' wasn't a word she could associate with the irascible figure who had dominated most of her life—still dominated it, if she was honest. It was because of him that she felt guilty if she wasn't always busy, working almost the same kind of hours that he had—and because of him that she had never had a boyfriend, when all her friends had been proudly parading theirs.

'You listen to your grandpa, child,' he'd used to say to her. 'Don't you let no one make a fool of you. If your ma had listened to me, she'd never have gone off with that damned rascal. But she was weak and silly, just like a woman—fancying herself in love and believing all his damned lies—and look at the way she ended up. But you take after me—a real chip off the old block. You'd never let yourself make a mistake like that.'

Was Margot right? Had he done too good a job of making her cautious, so that she had come to regard every man she met with suspicion...?

But she was right to regard this one with suspicion, she reminded herself crisply—his reputation was enough to warn her of that. And though the way he was looking at her over the restaurant table seemed to convey the message that he found her attractive, the spectre of that threatened takeover bid still cast its shadow. Until she knew for sure who was behind Falcon Holdings, she could afford to trust no one.

She cast a swift glance at her watch, surprised to see that they had been sitting there for over an hour and a half—where had the time gone? Catching the eye of the waiter to summon the bill, she turned to Jake with a smile of polite apology. 'I'm afraid I...have to be going—my chauffeur will be back for me shortly. Can I give you a lift somewhere?'

He smiled that lazy, sensuous smile, casually intercepting the waiter as he brought the bill and handing him his credit card. 'Thank you—a lift back to my hotel would be very handy, if it's not too much out of your way.'

It was, but she could hardly withdraw the offer. 'Of course not,' she assured him. 'And please let me pay for lunch—after all, I invited you.'

'You can pay next time,' he responded, a wicked glint in those deep-set hazel eyes.

She returned him a thin smile. If she had her way, there wouldn't ever *be* a next time—he had tricked her quite neatly into having lunch with him today, but in future she would be twice as careful. Rising elegantly to her feet, she swung her handbag onto her shoulder, waiting while he signed the bill and then preceding him through the restaurant, exchanging pleasant farewells with Henri as he held the door open for them.

The ice-blue Rolls Royce was waiting at the kerb, and Maurice stepped smartly round to open the rear door for them. She gave him the new directions and settled herself in the far corner of the leather seat, a little too aware of the uncompromisingly male presence beside her. He seemed to take up an inordinate amount of room, his long legs stretched out in front of him and his arm resting casually along the back of the seat so that his hand swung disconcertingly close to her shoulder.

'Why don't you get yourself a drink?' she invited, indicating the leather niche set into the bulkhead that separated them from Maurice. 'I'm afraid I don't have lager, but there's whisky and brandy.'

'I don't mind if I do,' he accepted genially. 'One for you?'

'I'll...have a small brandy.' She didn't really want one, but she seemed to need something to do with her hands.

The drink he poured from the cut-glass decanter could hardly be described as 'small', but she accepted it with a strained smile. The traffic was rather heavier than it had been earlier, and as they drew towards Trafalgar Square it came to a complete halt. She pressed the button to lower the glass partition between the front and rear seats, and leaned forward.

'What's causing the hold-up, Maurice?'

'Looks like a bit of a demonstration, miss. I'll see if I can cut down towards the Embankment and get round that way.'

'Thank you.' She sat back, glancing at her watch.

'I'm sorry—I've made you late for your appointment,' Jake remarked.

'Oh, it . . . doesn't matter,' she responded with a shrug of her slim shoulders. 'I can put it off to tomorrow.' Now, why had she said that? The last thing she wanted was to prolong this uncomfortable encounter—wasn't it? So why had she offered him a lift in the first place? a small nagging voice enquired mockingly. He could just as easily have taken a taxi.

Maurice knew most of the best routes through London, and they quickly found themselves skimming along the bank of the Thames, past the leafy Embankment Gardens towards the elaborate neo-gothic edifice of the Houses of Parliament, presided over by the imposing tower of Big Ben.

'Hey, this a real sightseeing tour,' Jake remarked, leaning over to look out of the window as they passed Westminster Abbey. 'Isn't Buckingham Palace around here somewhere?'

'Yes, it is, sir,' Maurice responded. 'We can go round that way if you wish.'

Georgia would have protested, but she could hardly argue with Jake in front of the chauffeur. Turning into Birdcage Walk, they drove down the side of St James's Park, and in a moment they were swinging round past the high gilt-tipped railings in front of the palace, with its ceremonial guards in their red coats and plumed helmets.

There were even more tourists here than there had been around the tower, basking in the unexpected bonus of sunshine in London. Suddenly Jake leaned forward. 'Stop the car, Maurice—I fancy a walk.' The chauffeur

brought the car to a sedate halt at the kerb, and before
Georgia had realised what was happening Jake had
grabbed her hand and pulled her out. 'It's much too nice
a day to go back to work,' he insisted. 'Let's walk in
the park. Come back for us in an hour, Maurice.'

'Very good, sir,' the chauffeur responded, his bland
face concealing any thoughts he might have had regarding this unexpected turn of events.

Georgia found herself on the pavement, watching in
startled amazement as her car drove away. 'I... What
do you think you're doing?' she demanded, furious. 'I
can't just go walking in the park—I have a great deal to
do.'

'Let your hair down, Miss Geldard,' he urged her
breezily. 'Old Grandpappy ain't around to tell you off
for slacking now.'

No, he wasn't she mused, feeling a little light-headed—
maybe she shouldn't have had that brandy. Whatever,
she allowed Jake to drag her across the wide road that
circled the ornate Victoria Memorial, planted like a
wedding-cake in the middle of a sea of ceremonial red
tarmac, and coax her over the low railing into the sweet
green paradise of St James's Park.

'Hey, now, this is really pretty!' he declared, gazing
approvingly at the long, curving lake, sparkling in the
sun. 'Why don't we take a stroll down to that bridge
and feed the ducks?'

Georgia laughed a little uncertainly. 'How did you ever
manage to become a business tycoon, spending your af-
ternoons feeding ducks?' she enquired.

'Ah, but that's the secret,' he assured her, mock-
serious. 'You've got to be able to relax a little, learn to
unwind. Feeding the ducks is what they don't teach you
at business school.'

He hadn't let go of her hand, but she pretended not
to notice. They must have made an incongruous couple,

she reflected with a touch of wry humour—she in her elegant jade silk suit and high heels, her hair swept into a neat pleat on the back of her head, beside this tall, broad-shouldered man with his casual clothes, tousled blond hair and long, rangy stride.

'There, now—isn't this a lot nicer than dashing back to a stuffy office and some stuffy meeting?' he teased lazily as they reached the bridge, drawing her over to the rail to look down at the ducks and moorhens scudding around busily on the shining water below.

'Yes, I...suppose it is,' she was forced to concede. It was certainly something she had never done before; for ten years she had studied and worked in this city, and she had never once taken a stroll in the park. It made her a little nervous that he had been able to persuade her so easily to break her routine.

It was like a little green oasis, away from the roar of the traffic and the baking heat of hard concrete pavements. A soft summer breeze whispered in the leaves of the trees, and the scent of grass filled the air. At the far end of the lake, beyond the sparkling play of the fountain, the white towers and pointed grey roofs of Horse Guards and Whitehall looked as if they would have been more at home in some Ruritanian fantasy than in the heart of London.

'Let's go sit on the grass.'

She knew she ought to call a halt at this point, insist on going back to the car. But the sun was warm on her face and Jake was still holding her hand. The spiked heels of her shoes were not really suitable for walking on grass, so she paused and slipped them off, carrying them in her hand.

'...a day for strolling barefoot in the park hand-in-hand with your lover...' She had laughed at Henri's words, but here she was, not two hours later, doing just that... Except that Jake Morgan wasn't her lover, she reminded herself a little shakily. Nor ever would be.

Finding from somewhere the strength of will to resist him, she drew back, trying to disentangle her hand from his. 'Look, I...really have to be getting back now,' she insisted, though her voice lacked conviction even to her own ears. 'My staff will be...wondering where I am.'

He laughed softly, mockingly. 'You seem to make a habit of going missing with me,' he remarked. 'Maybe that should tell you something?'

'Yes! That I should keep well away from you,' she countered heatedly. 'You're...dangerous.'

He slanted her a quizzical look. 'Dangerous? Don't forget, I saved your life once—all right, I'm not going to try to make you tell me what you were up to,' he added as her eyes sparked warningly. 'But it was hardly the action of a lady too staid and sensible to take half an hour off for a walk in the park.'

'I'm not staid!' she protested, stung.

'No? Then come and sit on the grass for a little while.' He threw himself down beneath the shade of a tall poplar, stretching out lazily with his hands folded beneath his head and his long legs crossed at the ankles. The glint of amusement in those dark eyes challenged her to sit down beside him.

Just walk away, the voice of reason told her. Don't let him tempt you. He's dangerous... But when he smiled up at her, her knees seemed to go weak, and she found herself dropping down onto the grass beside him, as if something else had taken over her will—something or someone.

There were lots of other people sitting on the grass: office workers in shirtsleeves and summer dresses, taking a little time out from the rat-race to share the contents of their lunch-boxes with the myriad bird-life in the park, and some couples, snatching a brief lunch-time tryst, wrapped up in each other to the extent of being almost oblivious to their surroundings.

But Georgia sat bolt upright, hugging her knees, tense and defensive. It scared her that she seemed unable to resist Jake's beguiling persuasion—she should never have let him talk her into coming into the park in the first place, let alone into lingering here when she had work to do...

Something soft brushed over her lips; he had plucked a long grass-head and was tickling her with it. Slanting him a reproving look, she turned her head aside, but he let the grass-head trail instead across her cheek and down the long column of her throat, to linger against the lapel of her jacket, just touching her skin.

'Don't,' she protested, brushing it away.

'Ticklish?'

She swallowed hard, conscious of the blush of pink rising to her cheeks. 'No, just... I don't want you to touch me.'

'I wasn't touching you,' he contradicted her, and then his voice took on a huskier timbre. '*This* is touching you.'

With the tip of his finger, he retraced the path of the grass-head, slowly, tantalisingly, across her trembling lips and over her cheek, down the neckline of her jacket... into the soft valley between her breasts. She became aware that she had stopped breathing, gazing down at him helplessly, captured by the strange spell he was weaving around her as he slowly let his finger slide beneath her jacket and along the lacy edge of her bra.

'That's touching you,' he murmured, as with nothing more than the hypnotic power of his eyes he drew her down into his arms.

Some part of her mind seemed to have retained enough sanity to recognise the hint of mocking triumph in his smile. But she was helpless to resist as his fingers tangled in her hair, wrecking the demure style as he drew her head down to his; she had known from the moment he walked into the restaurant that he had intended to lure her into this, and if she had really not wanted it she should have left right then.

But she wanted it. Her lips parted on a soft sigh, inviting the plundering invasion of his sensuous tongue into every sweet, sensitive corner of her mouth, and she closed her eyes, letting him lead her down into the unfamiliar labyrinth of physical pleasure, where she had always been so terribly afraid to venture.

The kiss went on and on, as the sunny afternoon and the busy park faded into oblivion—all her senses were focused on the taste of him, the touch of his hands, the musky, male scent of his body. She was lying along the length of his body, and his hands slid slowly down to mould over the base of her spine, curving her even more intimately close against him, nestling her thighs between his. Her breathing was ragged, every inch of her skin felt flushed and tender; moaning softly, she moved against him in unconscious invitation, aching with needs she had never known before, needs she didn't understand.

But she sensed that he was still in full control of himself, and she lifted her head, puzzled by his restraint. That lazy, mocking smile taunted her, and with a sudden rush of horror she became aware of their surroundings. How could she have forgotten that they were lying on the grass in a public park, in full view of everyone passing by? Her cheeks flamed scarlet with shame, and she moved quickly away from him, slipping on her shoes and rising unsteadily to her feet.

'I...have to go,' she choked out. 'I...Maurice will be waiting for me, and I...have an appointment this afternoon.'

He laughed with sardonic humour, rising beside her. 'Running away, Miss Geldard?' he taunted. 'Just like you always do?'

She turned wide, startled eyes up to his. 'Wh-what do you mean?' she protested. 'You . . . don't know anything about me.'

'I know more than you think,' he responded, softly, provocatively. 'You've been running scared all your life, afraid of what you might find out about yourself if you let anyone get too close.'

'Don't be ridiculous!' she countered on a note of rising panic. 'What on earth should I be afraid of?'

The glint in those dark eyes was disturbingly perceptive. He lifted one hand to her face, brushing the pad of his thumb lightly over her soft, bruised lips, and then he bent his head to place the lightest kiss there. 'I think perhaps you're just beginning to find out.'

CHAPTER FOUR

THERE was an air of hushed elegance about the Geldard's boardroom, in spite of the modernity of its decor. The long wall of windows was shielded by generous drapes of soft white muslin, the floor was covered in a pale grey carpet deep enough to absorb all sound, and the tubs of indoor palms were lush and green, expertly tended by a specialist firm who came in every week.

But what dominated the room, uncompromisingly out of place, was the huge Victorian-style portrait of the firm's founder in its heavy gilded frame. Georgia perched on the edge of the big oval table, regarding the portrait thoughtfully. She could vividly recall the painting of it; she must have been about eight or nine at the time, and she had frequently been puzzled as to why Grandfather had agreed to sit for a couple of hours a week for the man who came to the house with all his clutter if it made him so grumpy.

A discreet knock on the door heralded the arrival of her secretary, bearing the smart leather folders embossed with the company logo, containing papers for the board meeting, and she began to lay them out around the table. She was followed by Bernard Harrison, who had a worried frown deepening the lines in his forehead.

'What's wrong, Bernard?' she enquired.

He handed her a computer print-out. 'The latest share report. Falcon Holdings have picked up another three and a half percent of our shares.'

'Which brings them to...?'

'Eighteen and a half percent, give or take a point. And that's just their official holding—you know as well as I do they could be hiding behind other names.'

Georgia nodded grimly. Though the rules of the Stock Exchange technically prevented a buyer from using nominees to increase their holding secretly, in practice it could be extremely hard to prove. And then there was the ploy of taking over other companies with holdings in Geldard's shares, she mused angrily—companies like Linepaq.

'Do you think they're seriously planning to launch a takeover bid?' she asked.

Bernard sucked in his breath, considering his reply with his customary cautiousness. 'Not necessarily. They could just be building up an investment—Geldard's is considered good quality stock, with consistent returns. But it's not a risk we can afford to dismiss lightly. Will you tell the board?'

She had already asked herself that question, and now she shook her head. 'Not yet. I need to be sure who's going to be on my side.' She sighed, glancing up at the portrait of her grandfather. 'He used to enjoy nothing better than setting Uncle Lewis and Uncle Giles against each other, you know,' she mused. 'It was a kind of game to him, but I wish he hadn't done it. They hate each other so much, I can never rely on either of them acting rationally or in the best interests of the company if they think they can score some points off the other. That's become more important to them than anything else.'

'I'm afraid so,' Bernard agreed heavily. 'And George's decision to go into the property market just at the point he did, costing him overall control, has left us in rather a vulnerable position to a takeover predator. Sometimes I think that towards the end he began to get a little . . . reckless.'

Georgia glanced at him in surprise. It was the first time she had ever heard him say anything remotely critical of her grandfather. But unfortunately he was right; towards the end of his life, the Old Man's grandiose schemes had begun to get more than a little out of hand. Perhaps realising that he wasn't, after all, immortal, he had tried to leave his mark on the world by stamping the Geldard name over everything he could.

'What I can't quite understand,' she mused, 'is why we're being picked on at this moment. Our shares aren't particularly undervalued, and our recent record is strong. There doesn't seem to be a great deal of logic in it.'

'It could be any number of reasons,' Bernard responded seriously. 'A lot of overseas companies are trying to get a toe-hold in Europe at the moment, and Geldard's is a prime target for that.'

Her secretary put her head round the door. 'Georgia, the directors are beginning to arrive for the board meeting,' she announced.

'Thank you, Janet—please ask them to come in. And we'll have coffee right away, I think.' That would at least give her a few moments to collect her thoughts. Even without the news about the shares, she knew it was going to be a difficult board meeting to chair. Jake Morgan would be there—it would have been more usual for him to have sent a representative than to come himself, but when had Jake Morgan ever done anything the "usual" way?

But, on the whole, she had come to the conclusion that it would be better to have him on the inside; for one thing it would give her the chance to get to know him a little better, to work out how he operated, and for another there were certain legal restrictions on his actions as a director of a public company which, although they might not actually prevent him from getting up to any devious tricks, might at least act as some constraint—the Department of Trade and Industry did not look favourably on any suggestion of insider trading.

So long as he didn't continue with the ridiculous charade of pretending to be attracted to her—though he should have got the message clearly enough a week ago that that tactic wasn't going to work, when she had walked away from him in the park. Of course, she should have done it much sooner, but at least she had found the will-power in the end.

The directors were beginning to drift in, greeting Georgia in a manner that was mostly friendly, though often a little patronising. But then many of them had known her since she was a schoolgirl, and she had found sometimes that it could be to her advantage that they tended to underestimate her a little.

'Good morning, my dear—you're looking very fetching today.' Giles Aldridge was the son of her grandfather's sister, and as the only other surviving blood relative of the company's founder he regarded himself as having considerable importance—far more, naturally, then his long-standing rival, who was merely a nephew by marriage.

'Good morning, Uncle Giles,' Georgia responded, accepting the kiss he planted on her cheek. 'You're looking very well yourself.'

'Oh, I like to keep in trim, you know,' he acknowledged, proudly squaring his shoulders. 'So tell me about this new chap that's joining us. Australian fellow, I believe?'

'That's right. He's just taken over Linepaq.'

'About time somebody did. Old Harry's been losing his grip these past five years, and that son of his is worse than useless.'

'Coming from you, that ought to be taken as a compliment,' Uncle Lewis snorted as he strode into the room. 'Something fishy about it, if you ask me.'

'Not at all,' Giles argued, predictably taking up the opposite stance. 'Sounds like just the sort of chap we could do with around here. Bright, go-ahead, full of new ideas.'

'Hmph! Doubt if he'll even bother to come along himself,' Lewis grunted. 'Probably just send along a nominee.'

'That's all you know!' Giles taunted. 'As a matter of fact I've just seen him down in the car park. Dare say he's on his way up right now.'

'Have you met him yet, Georgia?' one of the other directors asked.

Every eye in the room turned towards her, but she was well prepared for the query, her features schooled into a mask of bland unconcern. 'Of course. As a matter of fact I had lunch with him a couple of weeks ago.' Just at that moment some kind of sixth sense warned her that he had walked into the room behind her, and, summoning every ounce of the will-power her grandfather had drilled into her, she turned to him, her face a smiling mask. 'Ah, Mr Morgan—I'm so glad you could make it,' she greeted him, coolly polite. 'Allow me to introduce you to everyone.'

'Thank you,' he responded, the glint of mocking amusement in his dark eyes warning her—not that she needed any warning—that she was dealing with a very dangerous opponent. 'But I thought I told you—when we had lunch together—that my friends call me Jake?'

'So you did,' she conceded tautly. 'Jake, then. This is Giles Aldridge and Lewis Chadwell...' She managed to complete the rest of the introductions, her jaw aching slightly from the effort of maintaining that smile of cool self-possession. Then, with a glance at her watch, she suggested they move to the table and begin the meeting.

'Well, gentlemen, now that we've all met, I would like to formally welcome Mr Morgan—Jake—onto the board.' She smiled, saccharin-sweet, in his direction. 'Strictly speaking, of course, the articles require that we take a vote before accepting him, but since you've all had due notice and no one has raised any objections, can I take it that there's no dissent?'

She glanced around the table for confirmation, and then moved on smoothly to the minutes of the last meeting. A few moments' discussion of a matter arising gave her time to sit back and regather her resources, and to covertly watch the man sitting near the far end of the table as he watched everyone around it.

She had seen him in a formal dinner jacket, in casual jeans and an open shirt—even, though she tried not to think about that occasion, clad in only a towel. Today, however, he was more or less conventionally dressed for a board meeting, in a lightweight business suit of impeccable cut, though it was lent his inimitable touch of individuality by the petrol-blue silk shirt he wore beneath it, collar unfastened.

Four different occasions, four different images. Who was the real Jake Morgan? A man who defied labels, apparently—a chameleon, able to change his skin to suit his purpose. She was going to have to be very careful. And yet . . . there was an odd kind of exhilaration in confronting such an opponent—her life, which had begun to seem a little dull and predictable, was certainly more colourful since he had stepped into it.

The minutes dealt with, it was time to turn to the main agenda. There were a number of routine items to be dealt with before they came to the most controversial point— a proposal to close down one small sector of the company that was proving unprofitable. It should have been a simple enough decision, but it had been the subject of wrangling on several previous occasions, and this proved to be no exception.

'I just can't agree to letting it go,' Uncle Giles declared forcefully. 'This company's never been in the business of short-term expediency. You've got a highly skilled workforce there, and that's an asset you don't just throw away. With a decent injection of capital...'

'Throwing good money after bad!' Uncle Lewis objected with equal vigour. 'Look at the figures for the past five years...'

'Those figures don't mean a thing. In case you hadn't noticed, we've been going through a major world recession. Once we turn the corner...'

The argument raged back and forth across the table, increasingly acrimonious. Georgia was just beginning to consider some kind of intervention when Jake cut in, his voice quiet but carrying enough authority to stop the combatants in their tracks.

'Do you mind if I ask a question? Why is production spread over three sites?' Everyone began to answer at once, but again he cut in with that underplayed hint of power. 'Perhaps I should have addressed my question to the chair?'

Georgia drew in a long, slow breath, as much to consider how to explain such a complex situation in a few sentences as to compose herself to speak to him. 'None of the sites on their own has sufficient room for expansion. One of them is sandwiched between a railway line and the motorway, one of them is next to a designated site of special scientific interest, and the third is right in the middle of town.'

'OK, so why not get rid of all three sites and set up somewhere else entirely? You have the freehold on all three.' He glanced through his papers. 'They're worth more than enough between them to finance such a move.'

'Thought of it, old boy,' Giles Aldridge put in. 'Couldn't get a buyer—not so much as a sniff. Bad time, you see.'

'What? Not even for the one in town? Surely that's a prime site?'

'Ah, well...' Georgia's eyes flickered almost unconsciously towards the painting on the wall. 'We have...quite an attachment to that building. It was the first Geldard Bakery, started by my grandfather.'

'I see.' He glanced up over his shoulder at the portrait—was it her imagination, or was it glowering at him? 'And anything of the Old Man's is sacrosanct?'

She felt a touch of pink rise to her cheeks; something in the mocking glint of his eyes seemed to suggest that he was including her in that statement. 'Of...course not,' she responded, a little stiffly. 'In fact there have been a great many changes in the past couple of years—we've sold off a number of subsidiaries and franchised the retail sector—but the Redford Road Bakery is...a little bit special.'

'Tell you what,' Uncle Lewis put in, changing his view of the newcomer as he sensed a potential ally against his old adversary, 'why don't you go and take a look for yourself? A fresh eye on the situation—that's what we need. Someone who isn't hidebound by tradition.' He glared across the table at Giles Aldridge.

'Good idea!' Uncle Giles concurred, manoeuvring as swiftly. 'And you could take Georgia along with you, to fill you in on the background.'

Georgia opened her mouth to protest, but a mocking glint from those dark eyes silenced her. Coward, it challenged silently. She had no good reason to refuse to go—not one that she cared to admit to, at least. 'It...might not be convenient for Mr...er, *Jake*,' she suggested, with little hope of a reprieve.

'Not at all,' he responded smoothly. 'I'd be very interested.'

'Very well,' she conceded, almost hearing the steel gates of the trap snap shut. 'I'll ask my secretary to check when I have a suitable time free.'

'Good morning, Miss Geldard.'

'Good morning, Jim. How are you? How are the grandchildren?'

The elderly gate-keeper beamed in delight that she should have remembered. 'Very well, thank you, miss. Our Tracy's starting at college in September,' he announced proudly. 'Business Studies.'

'Good for her,' Georgia approved. 'Tell her to come to us if she's looking for a work experience placement.'

'Thank you, miss.' He tipped his cap as the elegant Rolls Royce passed through the gate, and Georgia pressed the button to raise the window. 'Mind how you go, now.'

Jake slanted her a smile of quizzical amusement. 'The old-fashioned family touch?' he enquired, an inflection of sardonic humour in his voice.

'Geldard's *is* a family firm,' she responded with cool dignity. 'We pride ourselves on staying that way, even though we're now a public company.'

'Admirable,' he approved.

She chose to ignore his mocking comment as the car drew up at the entrance to the bakery, where the managing director, flanked by several of his senior executives, was waiting for them. He stepped forward to open the car door for her and she climbed out elegantly, exchanging pleasant greetings with him as she had with the more humble employee on the gate.

'And this is Mr Morgan,' she added as he unfolded his length from the back seat.

He smiled that big lazy smile, shaking hands with everyone genially, but Georgia sensed a distinct air of constraint about them. It was hardly surprising, of course—they knew the reason for this sudden visit. And they were worried about their jobs. Geldard's was one of the biggest employers in town—if the bakeries closed, what else would there be for them?

'I've arranged coffee for us before we begin our tour,' the manager explained, leading the way to his office. 'I thought you might like us to fill you in a bit first.'

'Thank you.' Her eyes were already filling her in, alert to every detail. The building was old, but of solid Victorian construction which promised many more years of useful service. But even she had to admit that it wasn't really suitable for modern mass-production techniques—the lighting was inadequate and there was evidence everywhere of a chronic shortage of space.

From beneath her lashes she slanted a cautious glance up at Jake as he walked beside her down the linoleumed corridor. To him, the place must seem like a museum; she could already guess what he was going to recommend to the board—closure. And she wasn't going to have a strong enough argument against it; as a public company, they had a responsibility to their shareholders—there was no room for sentiment.

But touring the bakery floor, speaking to the workers—some of whom had worked for her grandfather before she was even born—she found it hard to consider letting them down.

'This is one of our classic lines,' she informed Jake as they moved to a long conveyor belt. 'Golden Geldards. They're still produced in the traditional way. We use a wire-cutting machine to form and shape the dough, which gives us an irregular shape that rises freely in the ovens—that's what gives the biscuit its famous light, crumbly texture and home-baked taste.'

Jake glanced along the line to where the trays of un-cooked biscuits were being loaded by hand into the vast ovens. 'I see...' he murmured non-committally.

'Of course, we could produce far more biscuits by going over to an automated system,' she conceded with a touch of defensive pride, 'but modern machinery tends to result in a much denser, heavier texture. We're very proud that our product is unique.'

He flicked her a dry smile. 'Very good,' he approved. 'How well do they sell?'

She exchanged a hesitant glance with the managing director. 'Er...not quite as well as we'd like,' she admitted reluctantly. 'They're more of a luxury item, and unfortunately, in a recession, people tend to cut back on that kind of thing. We've gone into the whole thing very carefully, done a great deal of market research to be sure that we're placing them appropriately and at the right price. Our problem is our production costs.'

He turned to survey the room—a hive of purposeful activity with people in white coveralls and white net hats briskly moving about, each one knowing exactly what they were doing and getting on with it. 'It's very labour intensive,' he remarked.

'Yes,' she conceded tautly. 'But, as I said, if we operated in a different way the biscuits just wouldn't be Golden Geldards. And we have a highly skilled workforce here—it would be impossible to replicate that if we moved production elsewhere. Besides, the biscuit line is what made Geldard's a household name—it's what everyone associates with us. It could be very damaging to our overall market strategy to close it down.'

'You're in something of a quandary then, aren't you?' he responded, a hint of mocking humour in his voice. 'Well, let's go and have a look at the next place.' His tone suggested that he had already decided this visit was a waste of time.

'You don't have to tell me what you're thinking.' Georgia glared at Jake belligerently over her ceviche of salmon and monkfish. They were staying at the same country house hotel just outside of town where she had frequently stayed with her grandfather when she had accompanied him on business trips up here—it always used to amuse him that when he was a boy he had worked for the family that had owned the house then, doing odd jobs after school to earn a few extra coppers for his widowed mother.

'Now look at me,' he'd used to chuckle. 'Sitting in what used to be their best parlour, eating my dinner. I weren't even allowed in here back then.'

Jake slanted her a look of amused enquiry. 'Don't I?' he queried. 'I hope no one else can read my mind so easily—it would make them blush.'

Georgia felt her own cheeks flush a heated pink. 'I'm talking about the bakeries,' she responded, with as much cool dignity as she could muster. 'It doesn't make sound economic sense to keep them open.'

'Not in their present form,' he agreed, breaking off a piece of bread roll to eat with his iced stilton soup. 'But you're right about the workforce; they're a valuable resource. It's the buildings they're working in that are the problem—if you could put the whole operation under one roof you could slash costs at a stroke.'

'So what would you suggest?'

'Ideally, sell all three sites. But that clearly isn't feasible at present, so I suggest you concentrate the whole operation at Pound End.'

'But it's nowhere big enough!' she protested. 'And there's no room to expand—you saw that for yourself.'

'What I saw was a great deal of space being wasted holding stock that's tying up even more of your capital. Streamline your purchasing, fine tune your inventory control, and you can cut your stock levels to a quarter of your present levels—maybe even less.'

She frowned, a little startled by the unconventional strategy but forced to concede that it had possibilities. Of course, its success depended very much on the reliability of their suppliers and transport, but those weren't insurmountable problems...much as she hated to admit it.

'I still doubt if it'd be big enough,' she argued. 'And with the whole labour force moved over there there'd be a lot more cars to accommodate. That was the major objection the last time we tried to get planning permission—car parking and access. There's a primary school and a hospital on that road.'

'There's a strip of land on the far side of the railway line—it's too narrow to be much use for anything but parking. Buy that up, put in a footbridge and presto! Your staff can drive in the other way and you can extend your buildings out onto the present car park, just keeping enough room for the loading bays.'

'You make it all sound very simple,' she responded tautly. 'But what if the council won't give us planning permission again? And where's the money supposed to come from? The last thing we need at the moment is to extend our borrowing.'

'The council will agree if you push them hard enough,' he asserted with easy confidence. 'There are too many jobs at risk. And as for the money, that will come from increased productivity—as well as the sale of the out-of-town site.'

'Who to?'

'The university. They're looking for premises for an environmental research centre—where better than slap bang next to a nature reserve? And they've got an EEC grant to pay for it, so there won't be any problem negotiating a reasonable price.'

'And the Redford Road building?' she demanded, infuriated by his smugness.

'Economically, it ought to be pulled down for redevelopment.'

'But it's a listed building!'

He shrugged his wide shoulders in that characteristic gesture of unconcern. 'OK—so turn it into a tourist attraction.'

She blinked at him in astonishment. 'I *beg* your pardon?'

'A tourist attraction,' he repeated, lazily sipping his wine. 'It's practically a museum as it is. Why not let people come and see how the biscuits and cakes are made the traditional Geldard way? You could convert part of it into a coffee-shop, so they can sit down and try the goodies there and then, and also have a shop where they can buy them to take home.'

Georgia felt her jaw tighten. It was an excellent idea, one she wished she had thought of herself—and she was furious that he was the one who had come up with it. 'So that's what you're going to recommend to the board, is it?' she grated.

'It is.'

'What if I won't agree to it?'

'You don't hold an overall majority,' he reminded her, a glint of amusement in those dark eyes.

'And you think the board will follow your advice?' she challenged.

'I think they'll recognise that it's the most sensible course of action,' he responded evenly. 'And it would be one way out of the impasse those two stubborn old men have got themselves into, without either of them having to lose face.'

Yes, it would, she mused bitterly. It would also mean the workers could keep their jobs and the old bakery would have a new lease of life—not to mention becoming a wonderful advertising ploy for the company. But just because he was right it didn't mean that she couldn't resent his interference. Suddenly the delicious ceviche tasted like ashes in her mouth, and she put down her fork. Already he was moving in on the company, making his influence felt, taking over control—and he hadn't even launched his bid yet!

The waiter arrived to remove their plates, looking concerned when he saw that her starter was only half-finished. 'Is everything satisfactory, madam?' he enquired anxiously.

'Oh . . . Yes, perfectly, thank you. I . . . found I wasn't very hungry.'

He bowed himself away, returning a moment later with their main course. Georgia eyed her plate with little appetite—lemon-roasted pork had sounded tempting when she had seen it on the menu, but somehow she had lost all interest in it now. She accepted only a tiny portion of vegetables, waving the waiter away as he tried to pile up her plate.

'Surely you aren't dieting?' Jake remarked, tucking into his own Beef Wellington with relish. 'You don't need to, you know—not from what I remember.'

Her blue eyes sparked cold fury. 'How dare you mention that again?' she demanded, her voice ragged.

He laughed softly. 'It's no good trying to pretend it never happened,' he taunted, his voice taking on a huskier timbre as his mesmerising gaze held hers across the table. 'It was one of the most . . . memorable experiences of my life.'

Georgia swallowed hard, struggling to free herself from the spell. Too angry even to notice the startled stares of the other diners, she slammed down her knife and fork and rose to her feet. 'You are the most . . . *despicable* man it has ever been my misfortune to meet,' she declared tautly. 'Why can't you just go back to Australia and leave me alone? If I never saw you again in my life it would be too soon!'

And, snatching up her handbag from the floor beside her chair, she stalked from the room, her head held high, though inside she was wishing she could slide through a hole in the space-time continuum and disappear from sight.

The tears were starting as she reached her room. Fumbling with the key-card, she let herself in and threw herself on the bed, surrendering to the storm which had been threatening, she realised now, for some time—ever since Jake Morgan had walked back into her life that night at the May Day Ball, in fact.

And it had nothing whatsoever to do with what was going to happen to Geldard's, she acknowledged bitterly, and everything to do with what was happening to her heart.

It was nearly an hour before she stopped crying. Exhausted, she lay staring at the ceiling; her head ached, her throat was sore, and her eyes felt swollen and hot. Easing herself carefully off the bed, she padded through into the *en suite* bathroom to peer at her reflection in the unforgiving light of the mirror over the marble vanity unit.

Yes, she looked every bit as bad as she felt. Wearily peeling off her clothes, she ran herself a hot bath, swirling in a generous amount of her favourite perfumed bath-oil. She lowered herself into the soft green water, closing her eyes.

What was happening to her? How could she have let herself fall for a calculated charmer like Jake Morgan, when until now she had always been so heedful of her grandfather's warnings? But the memory of those deep-set hazel eyes haunted her constantly—and the way they had slid down over her naked body, assessing with every appearance of appreciation the firm swell of her breasts, the smooth curve of her stomach, the slender length of her thighs...

With a groan almost of pain, she succumbed to the temptation to let her own hands mimic the imagined caresses that had filled her fevered fantasies, aching to know the touch of his hands on her naked flesh, to yield beneath the possessive demand of his body...

If only she wasn't who she was. How could she ever trust a man who seemed attracted to her—how could she ever know if he was interested in *her* or her wealth? Not that Jake Morgan needed to be concerned about that, she acknowledged wryly—he could probably buy her out ten times over. And he *had* seemed to be attracted to her before he had even known who she was...

Although she didn't know for sure that he hadn't known who she was that night at the ball, an insidious voice inside her head whispered mockingly. It could all have been a ploy to disarm her long enough for him to gain control of Geldard's. And besides, even if he *were* genuinely attracted to her, it meant little—he had the same reputation with women as he had in business. He was a predator, a shark—and she had no defence against him. If she let him get too close, he would destroy her.

She felt a little better after her bath, but she knew she would still find it difficult to sleep—a glance at the small travelling clock she had put on her bedside table told her that it was barely half past ten. The warm night air drifting in through the open window was laden with the scent of roses, and the midsummer moon hung low in a sky of deep cobalt blue. Perhaps a stroll in the garden would help her unwind.

Fortunately she had brought with her a pair of cool silk trousers and a matching wrap-around jacket—one of her regular stand-bys on business trips to slip into in the evening when she wanted to relax a little. As it was dark, she didn't bother with a bra—it was unlikely that there would be many people about at this time of the evening, and anyway she wasn't going far.

Avoiding the main part of the hotel, she slipped down the back stairs and let herself out through the fire escape door. The gardens were quiet and peaceful; pathways of old brick cobbles wound their way around the flower-beds and under archways heavy with honeysuckle and climbing roses down to a large ornamental pond, where an artistically contrived waterfall tumbled through a picturesque rockery and several large koi carp, bright as jewels, cruised just below the surface in the shadow of the lily-pads.

There was a low stone bench to one side, so she sat down for a while; there was something restful about the gentle ripple of water over the rocks and the occasional soft plop as one of the fish popped up to the surface to catch a fly—it seemed to soothe the jangled emotions in her brain, calming her troubled spirit, helping her get things back into proportion.

It really was unlikely that Jake was particularly interested in her, though perhaps he had been a little piqued by the fact that the assumptions he had made about her that first time they had met had proved so totally mistaken—she guessed that he wasn't the kind of man who cared to be proved wrong. And perhaps it would be better, after all, if he *was* interested only in Geldard's—at least she knew how to fight him on those grounds.

She had no idea how long she had been sitting there beneath the stars, when the sound of a footfall close by made her look up, startled. A familiar figure moved out of the shadows. 'Oh, you...made me jump,' she protested breathlessly. 'I...didn't realise it was you.'

In the darkness she could still see the mocking glint in those deep-set eyes. 'A little late for a stroll in the garden, isn't it?' he taunted.

'I... No, not really. It's such a lovely evening, and the roses smelled so sweet. I thought a walk might do me good before I went to bed.'

'Afraid you might have trouble sleeping?'

'Not at all. I just...I...' Her voice trailed away as he sat down on the bench beside her, her mouth was dry and she felt oddly dizzy—and tonight she had had nothing to drink except spring water with her dinner.

'The last time I saw your hair loose like this, it was soaking wet,' he murmured, stroking his fingertips back along the line of her jaw to trail up over the delicate shell of her ear. 'It suits you—you should wear it down more often.'

She stared up at him, a small shiver running through her though she wasn't cold. She had thought she was sure that his attraction to her was feigned, but now, as she gazed up into those deep-set hazel eyes, everything seemed confused again.

'You know, I was told something very interesting about you,' he remarked softly. 'I was told that that air of untouchability is no illusion. Is it true?'

She felt a wave of heat colour her cheeks. 'Wh-who told you that?' she demanded raggedly.

He shook his head. 'Never mind who told me. It *is* true, isn't it?' There was no trace of mockery in his husky voice. 'You may not believe me, but it's never been a sport I've pursued—deflowering virgins. I could never see the attraction. But maybe there could be something to it after all. I wonder...?'

His hand slid round to cage her skull gently, holding her prisoner as his mouth came down on hers, his sensuous tongue flicking between her trembling lips, warm and enticing, coaxing them apart. And she could only surrender, all the rational reasons why she shouldn't swamped by the aching need inside her that only he could assuage.

He groaned softly, his strong arms sliding around her to draw her close into the warmth of his embrace, and as his hand moved to caress her aching breast beneath the soft, slippery silk of her jacket she heard his teasing, husky laughter. 'Ah, now this time you *aren't* wearing a bra, are you?' he murmured, his warm breath stirring her hair.

'I...didn't expect to meet you out here,' she protested raggedly, afraid that he might think she had done it deliberately.

'No? Then it's just my good fortune, isn't it? You have such perfect breasts—as ripe and firm as peaches, with such pert little nipples, just waiting to be touched...'

She didn't know how to stop him as his hand slid beneath her jacket, his touch warm on her naked skin. His long fingers were cupping the weight of her swollen flesh, the pad of his thumb brushing lightly over the tender peak, rolling it delicately between his fingers, arousing it to a taut nub that sizzled in electric response. His mouth moved hotly over hers, his tongue plundering the sweet softness of her mouth in a flagrantly erotic exploration, melting her bones...

And then abruptly he stopped. Bewildered and confused, she drew back her head to find him smiling down at her with quizzical humour. 'Now I'm in a quandary,' he mused. 'This is hardly the most suitable location for you to discover the delights of sexual intimacy for the first time, but I have a very strong suspicion that if I try to persuade you to come up to my bed, or to let me come to yours, I shall get a very rude answer.'

His words struck her like a douche of cold water, bringing reality flooding back. A scarlet flame of humiliation heated her cheeks, and she rose quickly to her feet, fumbling to straighten her disordered clothing. 'Don't...ever touch me again,' she choked out. 'I don't want you near me—I hate you.'

He sighed wryly, a glint of mocking amusement in his eyes as he lounged against the stone bench, his arms hooked lazily across the back. 'We both know that's not true,' he taunted softly. 'What makes you sick is being forced to admit that you want me to make love to you. And one day, Blondie, the time and the place will be just right—and then you'll have to stop running.'

'So far as I'm concerned, there'll never be a right time or place with you,' she retorted. And, turning him an aloof shoulder, she stalked away, only the strength of her will keeping her head up and her feet from running.

CHAPTER FIVE

IT WAS probably the most difficult thing Georgia had ever done, to force herself to go downstairs to breakfast in the morning, knowing that she would have to face Jake. She had barely slept, and, gazing at her own reflection in the mirror as she finished dressing, it seemed to her that her eyes looked far too big for her face, their expression strangely haunted.

Shaking her head to dismiss the fanciful thought, she swiftly applied her usual light touch of make-up, and then, picking up her handbag and drawing in a long, steadying breath, she left the comparative safety of her room, and made her way down to the spaciously elegant dining-room on the ground floor.

There were a few people there, mostly businessmen tucked behind their morning papers—she wasn't sure if any of them had been witness to her walking out at dinner last night. The waiters, at least, were a different shift. The morning sunlight streaming in through the tall windows, and the pristine white cloths that had replaced the sophisticated dark green ones used in the evening, gave the whole room a different atmosphere which made it easier to keep the cool air of composure in place as she crossed to the table where Jake was sitting.

He glanced up at her approach and she favoured him with an aloof little smile, ordering coffee and croissants from the waiter as she took her seat. 'Good morning,' she greeted him crisply.

'Good morning.' There was a hint of something that

could have been mockery behind his smile, but his manner was impeccably polite. 'Did you sleep well?'

'Yes, thank you. We're meeting with a Mr Johnson from the local planning office this morning, and then at one-thirty we're seeing a delegation from the union.'

'I have a copy of our schedule,' he responded, a sardonic note in his voice.

'Good. I've...given the matter some consideration, and I've decided to go along with your recommendations. I think the planning people can be persuaded to co-operate with us over the Pound End site, but they may be more concerned about what will happen to Redford Road.'

'Oh, I'm sure you'll be able to persuade them,' he responded in that lazy, mocking drawl. 'Just turn on that warm, personable charm...'

Her eyes flashed him a frost warning, but at that moment the waiter returned with her coffee, so she had to bite back her angry response. The croissants were still warm, breaking apart easily in her hand and melting the butter as she spread it on. She took a bite, regarding the man across the table with a suspicious glare.

'You're moving in very quickly,' she remarked, her voice carefully controlled. 'Gaining the confidence of the board, becoming so closely involved in key decisions when you've been with us for so short a time. Do you always take such an active interest in companies you have such a comparatively small investment in?'

That fascinating mouth curved into a disturbingly sensual smile. 'Sometimes,' he responded blandly. 'It depends on what the company has to offer.'

She met his gaze, her blue eyes cool. 'And what does Geldard's have to offer?' she enquired.

'Oh, a very great deal.' He smiled—a totally unreadable smile. 'It's one of Britain's top companies, after all—almost regarded as blue-chip. If I'm going to get myself a toe-hold in the Old Country, what better place to start?'

'A toe-hold?'

He shrugged his wide shoulders, lounging back lazily in his chair as he stirred his coffee, meeting her undisguised hostility with casual unconcern. 'It's a global market-place these days—no one can afford to isolate themselves in just one sector. And with Europe set to be one of the biggest growth areas, naturally I want to be in on it.'

Georgia took a sip of her coffee and another bite of her croissant. Maybe it was time to risk being blunt. 'Have you ever heard of a company called Falcon Holdings?' she enquired.

Those hazel eyes gave nothing away. He shook his head. 'No—should I have?'

'They've been buying up our shares. It's been going on for a couple of months.'

'And you think they could be about to launch a takeover?'

'I don't know yet. If they are, I expect we'll know quite soon—their stake's getting big enough to start rumours, and that'll set the share price moving upwards. I suspect they'll show their hand within the next few days.'

'And when they do?'

'I'll be ready for them,' she asserted grimly. 'I have no intention of relinquishing control of Geldard's.'

'Good morning, Georgia. How was your trip?'

Georgia returned Bernard a wry smile as she laid her briefcase on the desk. 'Oh, I think you could say it was quite successful,' she responded, her voice conveying as little emotion as possible.

It had certainly been a successful trip, business-wise—spectacularly successful. They had come home with the kind of package that would please everyone. The council had been extremely enthusiastic about the plans for Redford Road, the university had jumped at the offer of the out-of-town site, and the union, relieved that the jobs of the workers were safe, couldn't have been more co-operative.

She ought to have been delighted. The Georgia Geldard she thought she knew, the successful business-woman that everyone else saw, would have been feeling extremely satisfied at this moment—not miserable and confused and wishing that she could have jumped on a plane to Australia with a tall, laconic, hazel-eyed man who she was sure was her enemy, but who filled her dreams night after night with images that made her blush to remember them when she woke.

He would be gone for a couple of weeks, he had said. Of course, she had known that he would have to spend time there—he had a business empire to run, and though with the miracles of modern communication he was able to be in almost constant touch with it while he was away, that was no substitute for his presence.

Perhaps it was just that it had been so sudden—she had had no warning that he was going. On their journey home he had just casually requested, as they had reached the M25, that they drop him off at Heathrow so that he could catch his plane. She hadn't know how to react, and she was afraid that her eyes had given far too much away. As they'd drawn up outside the terminal building he had leaned across to her, and, placing his hand along her jaw, he had turned her startled face up to his and brushed her mouth lightly with his.

'That's just on account,' he had murmured, huskily mocking. 'Keep it in mind till I get back.' And climbing out of the car, he had walked into the airport—a long-haul passenger flying halfway round the world with only hand-baggage. The ultimate in travelling light. Just the way he travelled through life, she had reminded herself bitterly—unencumbered by heavy-weight commitments or inconvenient personal relationships.

Unconsciously she touched a hand to her lips, feeling them still warm from his kiss. 'Keep it in mind...' How could she help herself...?'

'Georgia...?'

'Oh... I'm sorry, Bernard, I was miles away.' Literally. 'What did you say?'

He looked a little puzzled by her uncharacteristic abstraction. 'I said, have you seen this morning's share report? It's just come in on the wire service.'

'No...' The company secretary's frown warned her that it was going to be bad news.

'Falcon have made a dawn raid on our shares—they're up to twenty-eight point three percent.'

Georgia felt icy fingers clench around her heart. She had thrown down the gauntlet at breakfast yesterday morning, warning him that she would fight any bid—and he had taken it up immediately. That explained why he had suddenly had to fly back to Australia, she mused bitterly; even for Jake Morgan, a bid for a company the size of Geldard's would take considerable organisation—and considerable finance. He'd needed to return to his own base.

Absently she strolled over to the window and stood gazing out over the densely packed jigsaw of the City spread below her to the yellow concrete edifice of the Stock Exchange, the heart of the world's financial markets. The game was about to begin—a game that was supposed to be conducted by strict rules but often wasn't. Could she win, against such a devious opponent?

It was a sunny day, and the sky was a clear, vivid blue—more like Bermuda than England, she mused, something tugging painfully at her heartstrings. Way over there, fifteen miles to the west, a silver aeroplane had just taken off from Heathrow and was climbing up into that sky. Of course it could be going anywhere—not necessarily Australia. But it was a reminder of how small the world was becoming, with Sydney less than twenty hours' flying time away. Not really very far at all . . .

'Georgia . . . ?'

She turned away form the window, smiling grimly. 'Bernard, I need to see the current share register, and patch every change through to me as soon as it comes in,' she commanded, once again the Georgia Geldard she had always been—the consummate businesswoman, fighting to survive in a tough world. Leaning across her desk, she flicked the switch on the intercom to her secretary.

'Janet, call all the directors and see how soon they can attend an emergency meeting. Then get me the bank on the phone, and bring me the latest reports from every sector of the company. Oh, and get me an appointment with the chairman of the Securities and Investments Board—I think it might be worth trying to persuade them to take a closer look at Falcon Holdings.'

'You think they're going to announce a bid?' asked Bernard.

'I'm absolutely sure of it!'

'Oh, good hit, Nige!' There was a ripple of polite applause around the field as the ball shot low and straight between the goalposts. The player swung his stick in salute, reeling in his pony to canter back into the line-up at the T-mark, ready for the next play.

'Good game,' remarked Robin Rustrom-Smith, leaning on the rail beside Georgia. 'We could win this, with a bit of luck.'

'Mmm,' she agreed. 'We'll have to watch out for their number three, though—he's very sharp.'

She drew in a long, deep, refreshing breath, sweet with the scent of horses and summer grass; it was another gloriously sunny day, with just enough breeze to lift the pennants that fluttered at the tops of the goalposts. Against the green backdrop of the tall trees that surrounded the park, the ladies in their silk summer dresses and the gentlemen in their military blazers and regimental ties made a colourful sight.

It was practically the first time she had been out of her office for a month, since the bid had been announced. It was a cash offer, which was unusual, and that made it harder to fight—whoever was behind Falcon was pretty keen to get their hands on the company. But she had prepared the best defence she possibly could, and with the share price soaring they would be forced to increase their offer. All she could do now was sit back and wait to see how high they would be prepared to go.

'There's a friend of yours over there,' Robin remarked.

'Oh? Who...?' she enquired innocently, following the direction of his gaze—and her heart almost stopped beating. Jake was standing by the rail on the opposite side of the field, casually relaxed in denim jeans and a checked shirt, in characteristic defiance of the semi-formal dress code—he looked as if he was at a Wild West rodeo, not a polo match in leafy Windsor on an English Sunday afternoon.

He had seen her, and lifted one hand in mocking greeting. When had he got back from Australia? She hadn't heard from him—he had made no attempt to contact her. And what was he doing here? It seemed impossible that it could be mere coincidence—but how had he known she would be here? Had he followed her?

'Georgia? Are you all right? You've gone awfully pale—you haven't got a touch of sunstroke have you?'

'I... No, it's... I'm all right, thank you Robin.' With an effort of will, she managed to regather the scattered threads of her composure. 'Ah, it's the end of the chukka,' she added as the timekeeper's bell sounded and the players laid their long polo sticks across their saddles as they rested their tired mounts.

It was the signal for the spectators to spread out across the field, treading down the divots of turf that had been skewed up by the flying hooves. As Georgia and Robin ducked under the rail to do their share the player who had just scored rode up and dismounted close beside them, arrogantly athletic in the slim-fitting polo-shirt that stretched taut across his wide shoulders and the beautifully cut jodhpurs of white hide, moulding his long, hard-muscled legs to perfection. Even the faint white scar across his cheek only added a dashing air to his handsome countenance.

'Hi.' He flicked his golden hair back from his forehead with conscious grace. 'Enjoying the game?'

'Not bad, old chap,' Robin returned, with a casual indifference that Georgia knew masked a dislike that had endured since the two men had been at school together; on Robin's side it was tinged with a certain envy of the splendid physique that painfully emphasised his own skinny, round-shouldered frame, and on Nigel's a slightly puzzled confusion that the man for whom he had nothing but contempt should be so much more popular than himself.

Now he slanted the smaller man a look of hostile resentment and turned his attention exclusively to Georgia. 'Did you see my goal?' he asked. 'It was perfect. I just saw the gap open up, wheeled into it and *thwack*!' He swung his stick in imitation of his masterly shot.

Georgia smiled, tolerant of his boyish boasting—she had known the Honourable Nigel Woodvine far too long to be irritated by his airs and graces. And in spite of what had happened between them that day in the stables all those years ago, she had always managed to remain on friendly terms with him.

On her other side, Robin made a sound that could have been a snort, deliberately falling behind them as he concentrated all his attention on toeing down an awkwardly twisted clump of grass.

Strolling along with the handsome Nigel, Georgia couldn't help but be aware of Jake Morgan moving with an air of casual unconcern on a path that would bring him inevitably into collision with theirs. She tried to divert a little to the left, but he simply changed his own direction.

'Good afternoon,' he greeted her in that slow, mocking drawl she had been trying so hard to forget for the past three weeks. 'I didn't know you followed polo.'

'I didn't know that you did,' she countered, struggling to maintain her cool façade. She was glad to have Nigel at her side, the Adonis of the polo circuit—though admittedly most of his fans were in the mid-teen age group; by the time they reached an age to leave school, most of them had discovered that the reason his friends called him Woody had little to do with an abbreviation of his surname and a great deal to do with his intellectual capacity.

'Er... Nigel, I don't believe you've met Jake Morgan, have you?' she managed, her smile brittle.

'As a matter of fact I have.' There was an odd note in his voice that made her glance up at him in some surprise. 'I'd heard you'd gone back to Australia, Morgan,' he added. 'Didn't expect to see you back.'

'Oh? Why should you think that?' Jake returned, his genial tone a taut veneer over an unmistakable hint of menace.

'Thought maybe you'd realised you were onto a loser,' Nigel responded, arrogantly self-assured. 'Decided to skip out without paying your debts.'

Jake's eyes glittered with dark anger, well controlled. 'On the contrary, there's still more than two months to go until...settlement date,' he countered smoothly. 'And I hope by then you'll be ready to pay *your* debts.'

'You two have a bet with each other?' Georgia queried, puzzled by the degree of animosity between the two men. 'What is it?'

'Come along, everyone, we'd better be getting off the field—they'll be ringing the bell in a minute,' urged Robin, scuttling to catch up with them, his enthusiasm to break up the conversation convincing Georgia all the more that there was something strange going on.

'What is it?' she reiterated, standing her ground.

'Nothing—it was...just a joke,' Robin insisted, his cheeks flushing a deep shade of beetroot-red as he took her arm, trying to draw her away.

'No, it wasn't,' Nigel argued. 'Never more serious in my life. Liked the look of that filly—reckon I'd better see about arranging stabling for her.'

Georgia shook Robin's hand impatiently from her arm. 'I want to know what the bet was,' she asserted, confronting the two men with gritty determination. Her suspicion was well and truly aroused. Almost two months to settlement date—which would be round about the time the sixty-day limit ran out on the takeover bid for Geldard's... Had Jake been boasting about it, backing himself to win? She wasn't sure if taking a side-bet on the issue constituted insider trading, but she'd be talking to her lawyers about it first thing in the morning.

Nigel laughed in arrogant triumph. 'Well? Are you going to tell her, or shall I?' he challenged.

Jake shrugged his wide shoulders, his hard mouth curved into a smile of wry humour. 'I bet him I could get you into bed before the Geldard Cup race in September,' he stated baldly.

'You...*what*?' She stared up at him, so shocked by the unexpected revelation that for one awful moment she thought she was going to faint, right here on the polo field in front of several hundred people. But one glance at the faces of the other two told her that he was telling the truth.

A hot blush sprang to her cheeks as the memory rose in her mind of that night in the hotel garden; she had assumed at the time that it had all been part of his strategy to gain control of Geldard's—although after the way he had kissed her she had almost begun to let herself believe that there could be just a tiny crumb of genuine attraction there too.

Well, now she knew—he had had another motive as well. Bitter humiliation twisted inside her—how could she have let herself be so stupid, so gullible?

'You despicable bastard!' she breathed in a savage undertone. 'You are just about the most loathsome form of life that ever slithered on this planet! If I had some slug pellets with me, I'd use them to exterminate you. And as for you two,' she added, rounding on Nigel and the hapless Robin, 'I thought you were my friends, but clearly I was wrong. If I never saw either of you again, it'd be about a thousand years too soon.'

She turned to stalk away, but Jake caught at her arm. 'Georgia—wait a minute...'

'Take your hands off me!' she hissed dangerously. 'There's not a single thing you can say that I would want to listen to.'

For a moment he restrained her, those dark eyes holding hers, but then with another of those wry shrugs he let her go. Blindly she turned and walked away, unaware of her surroundings as she stepped automatically around people in her path, not noticing the curious looks several of them cast towards her as she ignored their greetings. Acid tears were stinging the backs of her eyes, but she refused to let them fall.

Hadn't her grandfather warned her that men would always have an ulterior motive for approaching her? He had been more right than he had known. She had heeded his advice all her life—why had she suddenly let herself forget it, throw her habitual caution to the winds, just because one tall, blond-haired, wide-shouldered man had walked into her life? Everything about him had warned her to beware, and yet it seemed as though she had been helpless to control the waywardness of her foolish heart...

'Georgia! But *querida*, you are crying—what is it?'

She blinked in surprise as a strong masculine arm wrapped comfortingly around her shoulders, and glanced up with a watery smile into the face of an old friend, Juan de Perez. 'Juan! Oh, I... It's nothing. Just... I had something in my eye.' Struggling for a semblance of composure, she moved smoothly out of his embrace. 'You're here with the polo team?'

The handsome Argentinean chuckled, shaking his head. 'Not with the team, no—regrettably I am a little too old and decrepit now for playing polo.'

Georgia managed a light laugh. 'Nonsense, Juan. Old and decrepit—you?'

His liquid brown eyes sparkled flirtatiously. 'Ah, you flatter me,' he protested, not too forcefully. 'Come, were you leaving? You were not going to stay to see the last end of the match?'

She glanced around, realising now that she had been instinctively heading towards the car park. But why should she run away? That wasn't the kind of tactic her grandfather had taught her. 'Stay and fight,' he would have said. 'Show them how little you care.'

'Oh... No,' she responded brightly. 'I...was just going to fetch something from my car. But it doesn't matter now.'

'Then let us watch the game together,' he urged. 'We shall each cheer on our own nation, and fall out in bitter patriotic rivalry.'

Georgia laughed again; she knew that Juan wasn't the type to take a mere game of polo so seriously—he was a charming, light-hearted millionaire playboy, one of the few who could carry off the image beyond the age of fifty without beginning to look pathetic. But his easy manners and unthreatening attention were perhaps just what she needed at the moment, to soothe the hurt of her humiliation—and nothing could more perfectly demonstrate to Jake Morgan the contempt with which she held his reprehensible conduct. So with a smile she accepted the offer of Juan's arm and walked back with him towards the field.

The bell had rung to announce the start of the last chukka, and the players had all remounted and lined up at the T-mark, waiting for the umpire to bowl in the ball. And then they were off, a tangle of horses and riders, the target of their attention bouncing across the turf as they galloped full-tilt after it while the crowd roared its approval.

'I must make to you a small apology, on behalf of my son,' Juan remarked to her as they both applauded a very neat manoeuvre by one of the Argentinean players. 'César has admitted to me his reprehensible behaviour towards you. Ah, he is headstrong, that one.' He smiled with a hint of pride. 'I trust you will forgive him?'

Georgia smiled back at him. 'Oh, there was no harm done in the end,' she assured him, refusing to let herself think about the consequences that had stemmed from that unfortunate episode. She could well imagine that Juan had made the young man deeply regret his actions—in spite of appearances, she knew that he had an autocratic streak, and was quite capable of enforcing the most stringent penalty.

Not that his own example was particularly good, she mused with mild amusement—he kept an obedient little wife at home in Buenos Aires while he gallivanted around the world with some of the most beautiful women on his arm. But he was so charming that no one could take exception to him; even the men whose wives were reputed to be among his conquests seemed to regard him with friendly tolerance.

Those liquid dark eyes sparkled. 'Ah, you are very forgiving,' he chuckled softly. 'More so than he deserves. But enough of my foolish son—I prefer to talk of more interesting topics. Tell me what you have been doing since we met last.'

'Oh, working, mostly,' she responded with a rueful laugh. 'I don't seem to have much time for anything else these days.'

He clucked in disapproval. 'That is not good,' he asserted. 'Too much work and too little play is bad for the constitution. I shall not allow it. While I am in England I shall make it my business to distract you as much as possible. Let me see—tonight we will have dinner, and tomorrow we shall go to the opera...'

She smiled, shaking her head. 'I'd like to, Juan, but really...'

'Ah, do not say no,' he pleaded, leaning close towards her and speaking softly in that fascinatingly accented English that so many women found irresistible. 'You would break my heart.'

She laughed, a little unsure; in all the time she had known him he had always been lightly flirtatious in his manner towards her, but that was just the way he related to all women—she had never even thought of taking him seriously. But he had never actually asked her out to dinner before.

'What's wrong, Juan?' she teased, trying to lighten the tone. 'Are all the husbands in London keeping too close a watch on their wives?'

He chuckled, laying his hand on his heart. 'Alas, my reputation! But if you will not even have dinner with me, I shall know that I really am grown too old and decrepit, and I shall retire for ever to my estates in Buenos Aires and grow cattle.'

The self-mocking humour disarmed her wariness; after all, she had known him since she was about ten—he did business with the company and had been one of the few men to be on friendly terms with her grandfather. She would be quite safe with him. Besides, if Jake got to hear about it, it would show him that she had wasted no time at all thinking about him.

'All right, dinner,' she conceded. 'Thank you.'

'Thank *you*,' he murmured, lifting her hand and brushing the backs of her fingers with his lips, his eyes glinting with satisfaction, before he turned with apparent reluctance to watch the rest of the polo match.

'Ah, *querida*, you have done nothing but talk about this business!' Juan protested, smiling teasingly at her across the table of the fashionable restaurant where they were dining for the third time in two weeks. 'No more talk of this horrible takeover, yes? I shall become bored—and I hate to become bored.'

His eyes glinted a merry warning, and Georgia laughed. 'I'm sorry, Juan. I promise, I won't say another word about it.'

'Good. And on Friday you will come sailing with me, yes? I have a boat entered in the races at Cowes.' He held up his hand to silence her as she opened her mouth to protest. 'Do not argue—I will not permit that you

PLAY

MILLS & BOON'S®

LUCKY HEARTS

GAME

AND YOU GET

★ FREE BOOKS

★ A FREE GIFT

★ AND MUCH MORE

TURN THE PAGE AND
DEAL YOURSELF IN ➡

PLAY "LUCKY HEARTS" AND YOU GET. . .

★ Exciting Mills & Boon® novels — FREE
★ Plus a Simulated Pearl Necklace — FREE

THEN CONTINUE YOUR LUCKY STREAK WITH A SWEETHEART OF A DEAL

1. Play Lucky Hearts as instructed on the opposite page.

2. Send back this card and you'll receive specially selected Mills & Boon Presents™ novels. These books have a cover price of £2.10* each, but they are yours to keep absolutely free.

3. There's no catch. You're under no obligation to buy anything. We charge nothing for your first shipment. And you don't have to make any minimum number of purchases - not even one!

4. The fact is thousands of readers enjoy receiving books by mail from the Reader Service, at least a month before they're available in the shops. They like the convenience of home delivery, and there is no extra charge for postage and packing.

5. We hope that after receiving your free books you'll want to remain a subscriber. But the choice is yours - to continue or cancel, anytime at all! So why not take up our invitation, with no risk of any kind. You'll be glad you did!

You'll look like a million dollars when you wear this lovely necklace! Its cobra-link chain is a generous 18" long, and the lustrous simulated pearl is mounted in an attractive pendant.

NOT
ACTUAL
SIZE

The Reader Service
FREEPOST
Croydon
Surrey
CR9 3WZ

If offer card is missing, write to: The Reader Service, P.O. Box 236, Croydon, Surrey CR9 3RU.

NO
STAMP
NEEDED

refuse. You have been working far too hard—you will make yourself ill. I insist that you shall have a rest—absolutely.'

Georgia didn't argue. It was so nice to have someone who was simply concerned for her welfare. And he was good for her. She was so determined to fight off the takeover that she would have been working thirty-six hours a day if she could, but he had been there, coaxing and cajoling her to take regular breaks. And, though he really wasn't interested in the tedious details of it all, he had been there for her to talk to.

And there was no way Jake wouldn't know of her dates with him, she mused with grim satisfaction. Juan had a high profile in London—the tabloid press regarded him as exotic and therefore always worth a photograph, and he was happy to oblige. And tonight their table had been the focus of attention all evening, as friends and acquaintances, the famous and the infamous, came over to greet him. Some of them at least had known who she was, and she had been aware of a certain amount of surprise and curiosity that she should be seen out with such a notorious playboy when it was known that she didn't usually date men.

But he was so irresistibly charming that she couldn't help but enjoy his company, laughing at his outrageous flattery and letting herself begin to mind a little less about Jake's cruel treachery. And, although he had kissed her a few times, he hadn't tried to pressure her into a more intimate relationship, and she was grateful for that. Oh, she had enjoyed his kisses—there was no denying his expertise—but whenever she thought about taking the relationship further... Somehow she just couldn't begin to imagine it.

It wasn't like that with Jake Morgan, a whispering voice in her head reminded her irritatingly. You used to dream about his caresses—you still do...

'So, you have finished your coffee?' he queried.
'Good. Now I shall take you dancing.'

'Oh, but...' She shook her head. 'I can't, Juan, really.
I have to be up early in the morning—I've got a really
important business meeting.'

'Bah!' He muttered something in Spanish, which
Georgia suspected was very rude. 'Me, I am sick to death
of this business, business, business. I'll tell you what
would please me. Yes. That you should sell this damned
business after all, and come be my mistress. We will have
a fine time together, you and I.'

Georgia laughed a little nervously. 'Juan...
You...can't be serious. You're married.'

'That is true,' he responded, those liquid dark eyes
almost sorrowful. 'But my wife and I, we have lived our
separate lives for many years. We would divorce, but she
is a good Catholic, and so...' He gave an eloquent shrug.
'Of course, if it is a problem for you, I will quite
understand.'

'I...don't know, Juan,' she murmured. 'It's...very
sudden, after all the time we've known each other. Why
the change?'

'Sudden? Maybe. But who can lay down rules for these
things? The human heart is a strange, capricious thing.
Do not ask me to explain why on one exact day I saw
you and felt something I had not felt for you before—
if I could answer that I could answer the whole riddle
of human existence. It is enough for me that I feel it—
and I hope that maybe you feel something like it too.'
He took her hand, laying a kiss on the delicate pulse-
point of her wrist.

Georgia drew her hand away thoughtfully. Maybe she
could understand the change after all. Maybe Jake had
awakened something in her that had lain dormant, un-
suspected, for a very long time—and Juan, with his

acutely perceptive eye for the moods of a woman, had recognised it.

Perhaps it had been a mistake to neglect that side of life for so long, she mused—her lack of experience had left her dangerously vulnerable. And who better to gain experience with than Juan de Perez? If one tenth of the stories told about him were true, he was a past master in the art of love. And at least she would know where she stood with him, right from the start...

'You are smiling?' he queried gently. 'Maybe you are considering my suggestion, after all?'

She laughed, shaking her head. 'Don't rush me, Juan. I'd need to think about that one very long and hard.'

He acknowledged that with a slight inclination of his head. 'Think, then, *querida*. And then come sailing with me, yes?'

'I'll... let you know by Thursday morning,' she temporised. 'But tonight I really must go home early.'

He conceded on that minor point, clearly confident that he would win the major one. And as he drove her home in his sleek gull-wing Lamborghini—at a speed she suspected was well in excess of the limit—she knew that she was giving the idea serious consideration.

She was a little surprised that he had chosen to make her the object of such serious attention—she wouldn't have thought she had the usual qualifications. Maybe he really had gone through all the other women available, and she was the only one left? But at least she knew that he wasn't doing it just to win a bet, she reflected bitterly.

They had arrived at the stone pillars that marked the entrance to Larchwood, her beautiful home in the Berkshire countryside. The gates stood open—Maurice, who lived with his wife in the cottage just inside the tall hedge, would close them later, before he went to bed, as usual. The wide tyres of the Lamborghini crunched over the gravel drive as Juan swung the car around the well tended rosebed at the front, and drew it to a halt by the door.

The gull-wing doors slid smoothly upwards on their pneumatic struts, but Georgia waited as he came round to assist her to her feet—he had a delightfully old-fashioned attachment to such courtesies, and besides, it wasn't the easiest car to get out of.

'So, until the weekend,' he murmured smokily.

He must have sensed her wariness, because he didn't try to take her in his arms—he simply held onto her hand and drew her closer. His lips, warm and firm, moved over hers with a sure sensuality, the tip of his tongue probing into the sweet corners of her mouth, expertly coaxing her to respond.

So why can't I? she wondered a little desperately. Why do I feel nothing at all?

Because it's the wrong man, that insidious voice whispered back. You want Jake Morgan, and no one else will do.

Impatiently she thrust that thought from her mind. Juan had asked her to go sailing with him—and she knew that he would be expecting that she would agree to go to bed with him as well. And she would, she decided in a spirit of reckless determination, refusing to acknowledge the doubt, like a cold leaden lump, in the pit of her stomach. If there was one thing guaranteed to make her forget Jake Morgan, it was making love with an expert in the art like Juan de Perez.

'Goodnight, *querida*,' he murmured. 'Sleep well.'

'Goodnight, Juan. And...thank you for a lovely evening.'

She returned his farewell wave as he climbed into the car, the doors folding down into the sides and the powerful twelve-cylinder engine booming into life like a small aeroplane about to take off. She really ought to remind him about the speed limit, she reflected wryly, as she found her key and let herself into the quiet house.

CHAPTER SIX

GEORGIA yawned and leaned back in her leather executive chair. It was almost eleven o'clock, and she was still at her desk, but she had to get this report finished and ready for the printers tonight if she was going to be able to get away tomorrow to go sailing with Juan.

She had been trying to focus her mind purely on the sailing aspect of the trip. She would enjoy that—it was several years since she had been to Cowes for the annual regatta week, but she'd often used to go when she was younger, crewing for friends whenever she could. The other matter she had tried not to think about too much, ignoring her misgivings—she had made up her mind to do it, and she would. After all, why should she worry that he was married? He had had any number of affairs over the years—one more would make no difference.

With a sigh she turned her attention back to the computer screen in front of her, reading over the last paragraph she had written. With just a little over half of the sixty-day period to run, it was proving a tough battle; to her disappointment, the Securities and Investments Board had refused to block the bid—Falcon had made a good cash offer, and the bland young American whiz kid who represented them had argued a very convincing case that it was not in the interests of the shareholders to deny them the right to accept it. But she had received enough assurances of support to be quietly confident.

An unexpected sound in the outer office brought her head up sharply. The security guard on his rounds...? Her heart began to thud as the door swung slowly open;

some kind of sixth sense had already warned her who it was—there was only one person who would have the cheek to walk in here without knocking.

Jake Morgan was leaning one wide shoulder casually against the frame, regarding her with a faintly sardonic smile. His dark blond hair was falling loosely over his forehead, and in a white cotton shirt, the collar open and the sleeves rolled back across his powerful wrists, and lean-fitting jeans of faded blue denim, he exuded an aura of raw masculinity that made her mouth go suddenly dry.

'You're working very late,' he remarked, easing himself away from the doorframe and strolling across the room towards her without bothering to wait for an invitation.

'H-How did you get in here?' she demanded, trying for an air of frosty dignity but unable to keep her voice quite steady.

'Security let me in,' he responded, a wicked glint in those deep-set hazel eyes. 'After all, I *am* a director.'

Struggling to regain her composure, she returned him a withering look. 'I'm surprised you have the nerve to come here—I told you I never want to see you again.'

He laughed in lazy mockery. 'Oh, I checked for slug pellets on my way in. You have a splendid line in insults, you know—that one was particularly contemptuous.'

'Unfortunately it doesn't seem to have had the desired effect,' she rapped tartly.

'Well, no. But then you could hardly expect me to stay away—apart from any. . . other considerations, I'm naturally interested in what's happening with this takeover bid. I have to keep an eye on my investment.'

'Then you'll be pleased to know that we're fighting back very effectively,' she informed him loftily.

'Is that so? I heard you didn't make much of an impression on the SIB.'

'Well, no—but I rather expected that,' she countered, as coolly as she could. 'It wasn't the only plank of our strategy.'

'I'm glad to hear it. It must be costing you quite a packet, though, what with legal fees and bankers' fees and everything?'

'Naturally there are costs,' she returned tautly. 'But one expects that.'

'Does one?' he taunted, mocking her clipped tones.

'I don't anticipate any difficulty in arranging any financial backing I might need,' she asserted, annoyed with herself for letting him needle her.

'Good. I was going to offer you my support, but I don't suppose that would be...exactly welcome?'

'No, it wouldn't,' she ground out. 'Frankly, you're the *last* person I'd turn to.'

'I rather expected you to say that,' he conceded, his voice softly persuasive. 'You know, it's a pity you can't bring yourself to trust me—you have nothing to fear from me.'

'No? You call trying to seduce me in order to win some crass bet "nothing to fear"?' she retorted acidly. 'I'm sorry, but in my book that isn't the action of someone I can trust.'

He acknowledged that point with a wry smile. 'I suppose it would be a waste of breath trying to explain?'

'Yes, it would!' Why was she even letting him lure her into this conversation? She should have simply demanded that he leave and then ignored him completely until he went away. But ignoring Jake Morgan was easier said than done; her office was large, but with him in it, perched casually on the side of her desk, it seemed suddenly far too small.

He was examining the items on her desk with idle interest—a Victorian rosewood box she kept for oddments, a heavy soapstone egg that she used as a paperweight, silver-framed photographs of her godchildren. It felt like an invasion of her privacy, and she slanted him a look of sharp impatience, pointedly closing down the window on her computer so that he couldn't see what she was working on.

He noted her action with a dry laugh. 'Keeping secrets from me?' he taunted softly. 'You think I'm associated with Falcon, don't you?'

'Yes, I do,' she acknowledged bluntly.

He shook his head, untroubled by her response. 'Sorry—you're miles off the mark. You'd do better to ask your South American friend what he knows about it.'

'*Juan?*' She stared up at him, startled. 'Oh, don't be ridiculous! He's the *last* person I'd suspect of being involved in something like this.'

'Exactly.'

Georgia hesitated, momentarily taken aback. But then she shook her head dismissively; he was just trying to fog the issue. 'I've known Juan for years,' she responded with cool disdain. 'He's not the least bit interested in business—it bores him. He's only interested in things like polo and sailing.'

'Then you don't know him very well,' Jake returned grimly. 'He claims that his wealth is all inherited, but in fact the only thing he inherited was one medium-sized ranch in Cordoba, when he was nineteen years old. Now he's one of the richest men in the country—he owns thousands of acres of land, as well as oil and mineral interests and a substantial slice of industry. Hardly a mere playboy.'

'So?' she countered, arching one finely drawn eyebrow. 'Perhaps he's modest about his achievements. I find that rather refreshing, after the arrogance of some people I could mention.'

He laughed in lazy mockery, lounging full-length along the desk and propping his head on his hand, regarding her with sardonic humour. 'If you mean me, why don't you say so?' he taunted. 'It isn't like you to be so reticent.'

'All right—I do mean you,' she retorted, an odd flutter of panic in the pit of her stomach. He had invaded her territory—first her office and now her desk, overturning its neat, functional, businesslike aura with his disturbing maleness. Lying across it like that, he was making her think of other large, flat, horizontal surfaces . . . like beds . . . 'He's ten times the man you are—he's courteous and charming and gentlemanly . . .'

'A paragon of virtue,' he sneered. 'Have you let him make love to you yet?'

'No!' Her eyes blazed in hot anger. 'Not yet,' she added with deliberate emphasis. 'But that doesn't mean it isn't going to happen.'

'No?' There was a dangerous glint in those deep-set hazel eyes. 'It's been almost three weeks—it's unusual for him to be so patient.'

'I . . . I told you—he's a gentleman . . .' she protested weakly.

'Or maybe he hasn't succeeded in defrosting that icebox you keep your heart in,' he taunted, swinging himself lazily off the desk. She drew back in alarm, but before she could escape he caught both her wrists in a vice-like grip, jerking her abruptly to her feet. 'Does he kiss you the way I do?' he demanded, wrapping her arms around behind her back to imprison her as he dragged her roughly against his hard length. 'When he touches you, do you melt inside the way you do with me? And don't try to deny it—you may be able to play the ice-maiden with every other sucker you lure into your frozen realm, but I know how to send your thermostat way out of control, don't I? Or do you need a reminder of that . . . ?'

Her indignant protest was silenced as his mouth came down on hers in a kiss of fierce savagery that almost took her breath away.

At first she struggled furiously to be free, twisting and writhing in her efforts to escape him. But there could be no resisting that insistent demand—and deep inside her some treacherous instinct as old as Eve was urging her to surrender. There was something almost fatalistic in it; she didn't want to respond to him, but she couldn't help herself—he seemed to have some kind of power over her that she didn't know how to fight.

The last rational thought that slid through her brain was that even Juan, with all his expertise, somehow failed to have this devastating effect on her. With Jake Morgan, there was no possibility of a detached appraisal of the pros and cons—her heart refused to listen to any sense.

Her lips parted in sweet submission, yielding beneath the sensuous invasion of his tongue as it plundered all the deep, secret corners of her mouth. As he felt her yield beneath him he released her wrists, but her arms lifted as if of their own volition to wrap themselves around him and she curved her slender body closer into his embrace.

He had turned her back against the edge of her desk, his hand sliding slowly down over the length of her spine and then up again, savouring the soft contours of her body, moving with an intent that she recognised but didn't have the will to block. A slow, melting heat was coiling in the pit of her stomach, and as she felt his caressing touch on her aching breast she moaned softly, her back arching to crush the firm, aching flesh invitingly into his palm.

Suddenly the delicate lacy cups of her bra seemed far too tight, abrasive against the tender, ripening buds of her nipples, and the teasing brush of his thumb sent darting shocks of electricity through her nerve-fibres, making her toes curl. With deft fingers he had unfastened the tiny pearl buttons down the front of her silk shirt, was sliding it back over her shoulders, and her breath escaped in a ragged sigh as he released the clasp that nestled in the soft shadow of her cleavage, loosening the irritating constraint.

He had lifted his head, and from beneath her lashes she peeped up at him, her cheeks flushing as she realised that he was looking at her, savouring the nakedness of her creamy breasts, prettily tipped with pink; his hands were cupping their weight, his hard thumbs teasing the tender peaks, expertly arousing the most exquisite sensations. A delicious feeling of wantonness, of feminine sensuality was filling her, and her head tipped back as she moaned softly, her breathing ragged, her body curving towards him in helpless invitation.

'I haven't forgotten this,' he murmured smokily. 'The sight of you, lying naked on my sofa, has haunted me... taunted me...'

He gathered her close in his arms again, his lips moving over hers in tender enticement, coaxing from her a bewildered response. She moaned in protest as his mouth broke from hers, her head tipping back as she gasped raggedly for breath and he dusted scalding kisses over her trembling eyelids, her delicately veined temple, the dainty shell of her ear and down the long, vulnerable curve of her throat, to linger in the sensitive hollows of her shoulder.

He had lifted her skirt, his hands sliding up over her slender, silk-clad thighs, and her head swam dizzily as he laid her back across the desk. His mouth was hot on her naked breasts, circling tantalisingly over the ripe, aching swell, his languorous tongue swirling around the exquisitely sensitised buds of her nipples, his hard teeth nipping at them teasingly, until at last he took one deep into his mouth, suckling at it with a raw, hungry rhythm that pulsed white fire through her veins.

But just as she expected him to take advantage of her helpless surrender he let her go, laughing in teasing mockery. 'If you trust me so little that you're afraid to even let me see what's on your computer screen,' he challenged, 'why are you letting me make love to you like this?'

With a small gasp of horror she scrambled off the desk, scrabbling with clumsy fingers to refasten her disordered clothing. Why *had* she let him do it? She had no excuse, and the hot colour in her cheeks deepened in humiliation.

'Maybe you should start listening to your instincts, instead of trying to figure everything out in that clever little head of yours,' he suggested softly, and tilting up her chin he placed one last, light kiss on her warm lips. Then, without another word, he turned and walked out of the office.

As the door closed behind him Georgia felt her knees giving way and crumbled into her chair, tears streaming wetly down her cheeks. She brushed them impatiently away with the back of her hand. Damn him—what kind of cruel game was he playing with her? He could have won his bet, but he had chosen to simply walk away. Was he so arrogant that he believed he could take her whenever he wanted?

Apparently he did, and with good reason, she acknowledged bitterly—she seemed to have no defence against him. He had only to look at her, to touch her...

But she certainly wasn't fool enough to let her physical vulnerability undermine her business judgement, she vowed fiercely—and if he thought she could be so easily manipulated, he would soon learn his mistake. She knew he was the one behind Falcon Holdings, not Juan—the

fact that she was more susceptible to his kisses than to
Juan's had absolutely nothing to do with it.

She laid her hands flat on the desk, drawing in a few
slow, deep, steadying breaths. Tomorrow she was due to
fly down the Isle of Wight with Juan for the closing
races of Cowes Week. She had decided, almost cold-
bloodedly, to embark on an affair with him, and that
was exactly what she was going to do. Nothing had
changed—except perhaps that she was even more determined now to go through with it. That would teach Jake
Morgan to treat her like this!

The excitement began from the moment the signal flag
on the pole in front of the round grey tower of the Royal
Yacht Squadron's famous headquarters came spinning
down. More than thirty boats had been milling about,
but in the last minute they had all managed to turn in
the same direction, and now the tall sails billowed into
the wind and the sunlit waters of the Solent rose in curves
of white spray beneath the sleek racing hulls as each
skipper sought the advantage of taking the clear water.

Georgia, leaping to obey Juan's instructions, hauled
on the halyard to flatten the genoa as the yacht picked
up speed and slid into a good fourth place. The genteel
Victorian town of Cowes, with its ivy-clad houses and
gently wooded slopes, slid away behind them as they sped
like a flock of huge white birds across the sparkling grey-
green waters, seeking the first of the marker buoys.

It was a perfect day for sailing; the mid-morning sun
shone in a flawless blue sky, but there was enough of a
breeze to make for really good racing. Tucking an escaping strand of sea-soaked hair behind her ear, Georgia
drew in a deep breath of the fresh, salt-laden air, closing
her eyes to enjoy the sheer bliss of the moment.

She had made the right decision, agreeing to come—
it was just what she needed to refresh her brain, ready

for the tough closing stages of the battle to hold onto Geldard's. Flying down to Bembridge yesterday afternoon in Juan's nimble little Brazilian-built twin-engined Embraer, she had been more than a little nervous, not sure that she was quite ready for the inevitable development of their relationship. But she should have known that she needn't have worried—a smooth operator like the handsome Argentinean would never be so crass as to leap on her at the first opportunity.

He had booked a double suite for them at a smart hotel a short way out of town, close to where his yacht—the *Escaramuza*—was moored off-shore. They had dined on the terrace restaurant overlooking the sea as the sun had set in a haze of rose and magenta, sipping champagne and watching the spectacular firework display over Northwood Park. It had seemed like the perfect prelude to romance; perhaps she should not have drunk quite so much champagne as she had, but she had felt as if she needed it.

But then, just as it had seemed that the moment could be put off no longer, an urgent call had come in for Juan from Buenos Aires. She had no idea what it had been about or how long it had taken him to deal with it—by the time he had finished she had gone to bed and was in a deep, champagne-induced sleep. He hadn't joined her—she assumed he had slept on the yacht.

He hadn't been in the best of moods this morning, though whether that was because of the call itself or because it had interfered with his other plans, she wasn't sure. But with all the fuss of preparing for the race the incident had apparently been forgotten, and now he was in his element, his hand on the tiller, calling for minute adjustments to the sails as the wind or current changed.

The yachts were beginning to string out along the length of the course, the leader some distance ahead and probably uncatchable. But Juan's skill and seamanship were already bringing them up on the third-placed boat as they rounded the marker buoy and eased the genoa. The glorious multi-coloured spinnaker-sheet was hoisted aloft, ballooning in the wind and speeding them across the water as if they had wings.

The crew were kept busy, coping with the breeze as it gusted from gentle to fresh; lunch was thick sandwiches made from wedges of French bread stuffed with all sorts of extravagant fillings, eaten on the run as they skipped around the deck and washed down with gallons of champagne—but the fresh air and vigorous exercise had sharpened appetites, and the food disappeared with startling rapidity.

They had pulled up into second place by the time the last buoy was spotted, but another boat was behind them, pressing them close. Running fast under the spinnaker until the last possible moment, Juan was taking a risk— an awkward gust could round them up into the wind just at the moment when they most needed control.

'Stand by to gybe.'

'All clear!'

'Drop the 'chute! Sheet in the mainsail.'

The crew sprang to the winches, but Juan, his eyes on the rival boat creeping up on them, started bearing away a moment too soon. Georgia called out a warning to him, but for one critical moment the yacht heeled out, losing the racing line as they approached the buoy and allowing the other boat to slip through in front of them.

Juan let fly a stream of Spanish invective, but Georgia didn't even hear it—she was staring at the tall figure hauling in the halyard on the other boat's mainsail. Sliding past just feet away from her, he grinned wickedly, lifting one hand in a mocking salute.

What the *devil* was Jake Morgan doing here? Was he following her? It was surely too much of a coincidence that he should just happen to show up here at the same time. She frowned, a small grain of suspicion lodging itself in her mind; that phone call, the one that had kept Juan from her side last night—had Jake had something to do with that too? She wouldn't put it past him...

They crossed the finishing line in third place. Juan immediately handed over the tiller to one of his crew and went below, the hunched line of his shoulders eloquently conveying the state of his temper. Georgia sighed in wry resignation; so much for an exciting weekend of yacht-racing and romance—so far it was proving a dismal failure!

Georgia had been looking forward to the evening; it was the last night of Regatta Week and they were due to attend a ball at one of the yacht clubs. But between having Juan in a foul mood and her own anxiety about running into Jake again it was with some apprehension that she put the finishing touches to her make-up, stroking on just a hint of dark blue mascara to highlight the blue of her eyes.

She glanced up, startled, as the door opened abruptly, and Juan, elegant as a peacock in a white dinner jacket and scarlet silk shirt, marched into the room. 'Don't you believe in knocking?' she queried mildly as she carefully tissued off the mascara she had smudged across her cheek.

'I have been down to the Regatta Centre—I have put in a protest about the action of those *locos* who tried to run me down at the last buoy,' he declared fiercely. 'Defrauders! They think I will just lie down and accept it? They may think again!' He began to pace around the room, muttering under his breath, but then stopped abruptly, shooting his cuff to glance at the diamond-encrusted watch on his wrist. 'But it is late. Come, *querida*—you are looking exceptionally beautiful tonight. Let us go to the ball and dance the night away, yes?'

She smiled, relieved that he at least seemed willing to put the events of the day behind him; it was pointless trying to argue that the other yacht had not been at fault—irritating as that was. She picked up her long-fringed silk shawl and let him wrap it around her shoulders. His breath was warm against the nape of her neck, from where she had swept her hair up into an elegant twist on top of her head.

'Or maybe we shall forget the ball and stay here,' he murmured, his voice low and husky. 'I so much want to make love to you, it is driving me crazy.'

Georgia laughed a little nervously. 'Oh, but…I've been looking forward to the ball,' she protested. 'I bought this dress specially for it.'

'And an exquisite dress it is,' he approved, his liquid dark eyes sliding down over the low-cut sheath of blue-green silk with its unusual bustled skirt—the work of one of her favourite designers. 'But where are your famous diamonds?'

'Oh, Juan! I only wear those when I absolutely have to. Besides, it's such a bother, being followed around by a bodyguard all the time.'

She frowned slightly at her own reflection. Why had she lied to Juan? In fact the diamonds had been sold, along with the yacht, leaving her a reasonably good balance after paying off the loans. She had been a little surprised to receive such a good offer so quickly—the sale had been very discreet. But there was no reason why Juan shouldn't know… Had Jake Morgan's insinuations affected her, even though she had rejected them?

Juan laughed. 'Very well, *querida*, you *shall* go to the ball! And I shall be your Prince Charming, yes? Come, sweet Cinderella, your carriage awaits!'

Somehow she managed a smile, though a hard knot of tension had clenched in her stomach. The way he had looked at her, as if already mentally peeling off the dress, had made her go cold. And later tonight, when they returned from the ball, he would expect that she would let him do just that...

Of course, it was only natural that she should have some reservations, she reassured herself a little desperately—quite apart from the fact that it was something she had never done before, there was also the minor detail that he was married. It was all very well for him to say that he and his wife led separate lives; she couldn't quite feel comfortable about it.

She seemed to be moving in some kind of dream. The hotel's courtesy car drove them the short distance to the yacht club headquarters, housed in one of the elegant old Victorian buildings looking out over the harbour, but she was barely aware of her surroundings. She could think only of that moment in the hotel bedroom, and her reaction to it; it had had nothing whatsoever to do with guilt about him being married—she just didn't want him to make love to her.

The dream turned into a nightmare almost the moment she walked into the grand wood-panelled ballroom with its old-fashioned brass chandeliers. It was already crowded, but the first person she saw, on the far side of the room, was Jake Morgan.

He was wearing a formal dark dinner jacket again, beautifully tailored to mould the handsome width of his shoulders, and his dark-blond hair caught the light, making it hard not to notice him. He was talking to some bright young thing in a gown of doll-pink satin, cut ridiculously low over her generous bosom—and he was clearly far too absorbed in what she was saying even to glance up.

'Champagne, *querida*?' Juan purred, close to her ear.

'Oh, er...yes, please,' she responded with determined gaiety, turning her back on the man across the room—though she couldn't resist one last glance over her shoulder to check if he had noticed her arrival.

Why on earth had she come here anyway? It wasn't the sort of occasion she particularly cared for—there were too many people, all dolled up to the nines and greeting each other with phoney warmth. Keeping her smile in place was making the muscles of her face ache, but she had to look as if she was having a simply wonderful time—she was determined not to let Jake see that she was even remotely bothered by his presence.

If he had come to Cowes in pursuit of her, he was showing little sign of it—every time she happened to glance casually in his direction he was talking to or dancing with some female or other—usually the one in that silly pink dress. He knew she was there all right—once or twice he had glanced up and caught her eye, had smiled that infuriatingly arrogant smile, as if he thought she cared that he hadn't come over to say hello or to ask for a single dance.

As a matter of fact, she wished he *would* ask her to dance—just so that she could have the pleasure of refusing him. She was enjoying herself perfectly well, dancing with Juan—he was an excellent dancer, if a little flamboyant, twirling her around the floor as the seven-piece band played waltzes and tangos and even a little rock and roll, to satisfy the tastes of every age-group present.

'You are frowning, *querida*,' Juan remarked, smiling down at her in concern. 'What is it?'

'Oh, I...' She shook her head quickly. 'I'm sorry, Juan. It's nothing—just a slight headache, that's all.'

'You would like to sit down for a while? Or maybe to return to the hotel?'

'Oh, no—no,' she responded quickly forcing a bright smile. 'I'll be fine.' The last thing she wanted was to return to the hotel... Oh, Lord, what was she going to do about that? How could she tell him that she had changed her mind? 'Did you... er... manage to sort out that problem that cropped up last night?' she remarked, changing the subject.

His handsome face darkened. 'Oh—that! A minor difficulty, nothing more. I am sorry it took me so long to deal with, *querida*—especially as it kept me from your arms. But tonight, nothing shall keep me from you.'

He drew her closer against him, so that she had to turn her head slightly to avoid breathing in too much of his rather powerful aftershave—and she found herself looking up into a pair of mocking hazel eyes, which glinted at her in sardonic amusement above the head of his current partner, who appeared to be wrapped around him like an octopus with all its tentacles.

Quickly she turned away, startling Juan by resisting his lead and making him change direction to move towards the other side of the dance-floor. 'Was it your wife?' she enquired brightly.

'I beg your pardon?'

'Your call—last night.'

'Ah! No, *querida*,' he assured her, smiling. 'Just business.'

'I didn't think you took much interest in business?' she queried, feigning surprise.

'I do not,' he confirmed. 'It bores me.'

'And yet... I've heard that you're very successful,' she probed, carefully concealing her interest behind a flirtatiously teasing manner. 'I suspect that you've been hiding your light under a bushel.'

A look of annoyance flickered across his face. 'Who told you that?' he demanded.

'Oh, you know,' she responded, shrugging her slender shoulders in a gesture of casual dismissal. 'City gossip, that's all.'

His hold on her tightened, and his jaw clenched in unmistakable anger. 'I do not like that I should be the subject of City gossip,' he hissed. 'Tell me who told you.'

She laughed a little unsteadily, startled at his reaction. 'Oh, really, Juan—I can't remember,' she protested. 'It could have been any number of people.'

It appeared to cost him some effort of will to get his anger back under control, but then he smiled. 'I am sorry, *querida*, it is just that careless talk can so often be mistaken—as in this case—and yet it can be very difficult to correct. Come, I believe it is time we went down to dinner.'

She allowed him to lead her from the dance-floor, her mind working overtime. His denial had been unconvincing—it appeared that Jake's information about his business activities had been accurate. Not that that proved anything, she reminded herself cautiously—many people in the higher echelons of the international financial community liked to be discreet about their wealth. It didn't mean that Jake's other accusations were correct.

There had already been one sitting for dinner, but the staff had cleared away in record time and the dining-room was looking very elegant, the round tables covered in long white cloths, each one with a charming centre-piece of candles and flowers. White-liveried waiters moved around the room, quietly serving a feast of smoked salmon in soured cream with caviar, followed by lamb steaks in a caper sauce and rounded off with an old-fashioned trifle fairly soused in sherry.

They were sharing a table with six people she didn't know, and Juan was quickly embroiled in a vigorous debate about the value of epoxy resin as against the traditional method of caulking. She was relieved that she didn't have to make the effort to maintain a flow of scintillating conversation—she was all too miserably aware of Jake Morgan, just three tables away from them, with the girl in the doll-pink dress, apparently enjoying himself far more than she was.

She knew that she was drinking too much champagne again—she rarely touched alcohol, so it was going to her head very quickly. Somehow the entire weekend had gone wrong—and she had a strong suspicion that Jake Morgan was behind most of it. Though he wasn't behind her realisation that she couldn't sleep with Juan, she acknowledged miserably—she had really known that all along, though she had obstinately chosen not to acknowledge it.

Quite how she was going to tell Juan that she didn't want to sleep with him after all, she wasn't sure—but she was going to have to think of something soon. The evening was wearing on, and she couldn't leave it until they got back to the hotel. But the champagne was fogging her brain, so that the harder she tried to focus on the problem the more it seemed to slip from her grasp...

CHAPTER SEVEN

IT WAS hot in the ballroom—hot and crowded—and the lights of the chandeliers swinging from the high ceiling seemed to be going round and round. Georgia would have liked to go home, but she didn't dare suggest it—not until she had worked up the courage to tell Juan that she didn't want to share that big, comfortable double bed with him.

'Georgie! Darling, how lovely to see you! I didn't know you were coming over! You wicked thing, why didn't you tell me? Or can I guess? I've been hearing a little gossip about you lately—and I'm absolutely delighted. It's about time—and Juan is a darling!'

Georgia laughed as she kissed her old friend's cheek. 'Hello, Margot. You're looking well. I've no need to introduce you to Jaun de Perez, have I?'

Margot shook her head, her eyes slanting the handsome Argentinean an outrageously flirtatious glance as he joined them. 'Of course not!' she purred. 'Hello, Juan!'

'*Querida*,' he murmured softly, leaning close to her so as to obtain the finest view of her deep cleavage. He whispered something in Spanish into her ear, making her giggle in delight.

'Oh, Juan—you naughty thing!' she protested, a little louder than was necessary. 'You'll have to watch him, Georgie—he's an absolute rat!'

'Unfair,' he countered, his hand on his heart. 'It is that I am the everlasting romantic—I cannot help but fall in love.'

'And fall out of it again just as quickly,' Margot chided, mock-severe. 'Oh, look—there's my brother Robin. I must go and say hello—he'll think I'm sulking because Great Aunt Em left him *all* her money and me only a load of the most hideous jewellery. But he deserves it really, dear boy—he sucked up to her for years, and I just couldn't bring myself to. Bye, Georgie—see you soon!'

Juan turned to Georgia with a tragi-comic expression. 'Ah, now she has ruined my reputation,' he sighed. 'But do not look so serious, *querida*. We can only live for the moment, after all—no? Come, smile for me. Ah, you have finished your champagne. Another glass?'

Before she could refuse, he had stopped a passing waiter and exchanged her empty glass for a full one. She was beginning to feel a little desperate; if only she really was Cinderella, and at the stroke of midnight could run away—though she would be very careful not to leave behind a glass slipper.

Jake had come back into the room; he was dancing with that girl in the doll-pink dress again, his arm around her waist, holding her a good deal closer than was necessary. She looked little more than a teenager, all dewy eyes and simpering smile. Well, if that was the sort he liked . . .

'I want to dance,' she announced abruptly.

Juan looked a little disappointed. 'I thought perhaps you might be ready to go back to the hotel?' he murmured, his voice taking on a husky, meaningful timbre.

'Not yet.' She drained her champagne glass in one draught and, taking Juan's hand, wove a little unsteadily out onto the dance-floor. The room was a kaleidoscope of colour, drifting around her as if she was on a merry-go-round, and it occurred to her that she was probably drunk—which was not the best condition in which to consider how to deal with the problems ahead.

But she didn't care—it would serve Jake right if she *did* sleep with Juan!

Juan had drawn her close against him, his head bent over hers, his warm breath stirring her hair as he whispered into her ear. 'Come away with me, my love—be my mistress. I will make love to you on a gondola drifting silently through the misty canals of Venice, on an island in the warm Pacific Ocean, on a mountain in far Tibet. We will be lovers of the flesh and of the spirit. I will show you pleasures beyond anything you have ever imagined. I will awaken you to the world of the senses . . .'

She laughed a little nervously, trying to draw away from him. 'Juan!'

'I mean it, *querida*,' he husked, sliding his hand down the length of her spine. 'I am going crazy for you. I will tell you what you will do—you will sell this damned company of yours and we will forget the whole world. We will jump on an aeroplane to some exotic paradise where we will make love day and night . . .'

Everything happened so swiftly that she didn't really have time to see how it started. Someone moving past Juan with two glasses of champagne seemed to jostle against him, and the champagne was spilled over his pristine white jacket. He turned with an angry word, voices were raised and someone threw a punch—and the next moment there was a mêlée involving five or six people.

Georgia screamed, struggling to get back out of the way as fists flew wildly—and suddenly there was a protective presence at her side, drawing her back, sheltering her from the danger. She blinked in befuddled confusion as she found herself by the wide double doors of the ballroom, with Jake.

'I think you've had a little too much to drink,' he remarked with mild amusement. 'I'd better take you home.'

'But...Juan,' she protested weakly.

'I think you'll find he's going to be...otherwise engaged for the rest of the night,' he responded, standing aside as three policemen, one of them talking into his two-way radio, hurried past them. 'You seem to have some kind of aura that starts men fighting around you—this is the second time it's happened in my short acquaintance with you.'

She stared up at him, anger and suspicion surfacing through the haze of alcohol in her brain. '*You* made it happen,' she accused him. 'It's all your fault.'

'Me?' His look of innocence would have fooled no one. 'I was nowhere near them when they started fighting.'

'No, but...you were behind it somehow,' she insisted, frowning as she tried to focus her thoughts. 'What are you doing here anyway? First you turned up at that polo match and now you're here. I never told you I was coming. You're following me—I don't want you following me.'

He smiled crookedly down at her. 'I'm sorry to disappoint you, but it isn't you I'm following. It's de Perez.'

She shook her head, her confusion only deepened by his explanation. 'You're following Juan? But...why?'

He laughed in gentle mockery. 'I think the explanation might be a little too complicated for you at the moment,' he teased. 'Suffice it to say that I have my reasons. Saving you from the consequences of your own stubborn folly was just a bonus.'

'I didn't need saving from anything,' she retorted, with what she hoped was suitably icy dignity.

More police had arrived by now, and Jake drew her away from the doorway as they began to bring out the battered combatants from the ballroom, hustling them across the foyer to the police van waiting outside. Juan, protesting furiously, didn't even notice her as he was led past between two burly constables; he already had the start of what promised to be a spectacular black eye, and his elegant white suit was spattered with blood.

'What will happen to them?' Georgia asked anxiously as she watched them go.

'Oh, I dare say they'll just be kept in the cells over-night to cool off, and then be let off in the morning with a caution,' Jake responded on an inflection of dry humour. 'I imagine the police here are used to Hooray Henrys letting off a bit of steam during the Regatta Week—they don't take it too seriously.'

'Juan isn't a Hooray Henry,' Georgia countered, turning on him with an angry glare. 'Though I dare say you didn't have too much trouble finding one you could persuade to pick on him, just to start a fight and make this happen.'

'And aren't you glad I did?' he returned smoothly. 'Otherwise, about now you'd be on your way back to your hotel with him—and from the look on your face, you were beginning to regard that as a fate worse than death!'

'You're just jealous!' she threw at him bitterly.

He merely laughed. 'I would have been, if I'd thought you'd have enjoyed it,' he taunted, those beguiling hazel eyes glinting. 'But you wouldn't, you know. And frankly, I doubt if poor de Perez would have either—the state you're in, you wouldn't have done much but lie there like a sack of potatoes anyway.'

It gave her an enormous amount of satisfaction to find that though she was every bit as drunk as he had so insultingly implied she could still aim a good, straight slap that caught him square across the cheek, leaving the imprint of her palm in glorious scarlet. And, turning, she stalked magnificently away—an effect somewhat marred when she tripped on the step, almost falling over.

'Damn!' She had broken the heel of her shoe, as she discovered when she tried to walk on and found herself listing hard to port. Pausing, she discreetly slipped both shoes off and picked them up, his mocking laughter following her as she walked out into the night, carrying them in her hands.

Georgia rolled over in bed, groaning and trying to bury her head beneath the pillow. The sound tearing at her ears, that she had thought was of a thousand cats being systematically strangled, resolved itself into the squalling of the seagulls, and the hot yellow glare of a blast-furnace was merely the sun behind the curtains. Her tongue tasted as if she had used it to clean out the drains, and she had the very uncomfortable feeling that if she tried to move she would be very sick.

The events of the previous night were an unpleasant blur, the fact that she had to be grateful to Jake that she wasn't having to face the even more horrendous experience of waking up beside Juan this morning only made it all the more excruciatingly embarrassing. She remembered that he had followed her home last night, at a discreet distance, just to make sure that she was safe; in spite of everything, the thought gave her a warm little glow—until she remembered the blonde in the doll-pink dress.

Had he gone back to her afterwards? Damn him, why did she care so much? She wasn't going to let herself fall in love with him. Even if she was beginning to question whether it *was* Juan after all who was the evil eminence behind Falcon Holdings, she was a long way from allowing herself to trust Jake. There was the little matter of that bet, for a start. Her grandfather had been right—she had been far safer having nothing to do with men.

Maybe she was more her mother's daughter than she had ever cared to believe, she mused unhappily. She had managed to keep that treacherous vulnerability under control for a long time, but in the end she had started to make exactly the same mistakes. And she had even followed her mother's pattern in trying to drown her sorrows in alcohol.

Well, at least she had the sense not to let herself slip into that dangerous habit, she vowed resolutely, groaning as she tried to sit up—she was never, ever going to have another glass of champagne as long as she lived.

'Bodyguards? Oh, come on—that really is taking the whole thing too far!' Georgia glared up at Jake from behind her desk. 'It's ridiculous to suppose that I'm in any danger from Juan—besides, if he'd wanted to do me any harm he had the perfect opportunity while we were in Cowes last weekend.'

Jake shook his head. 'Too obvious,' he argued. 'He wouldn't want to take the risk of being implicated himself in any way. That wouldn't serve his purpose at all. Look, it's just a sensible precaution. I'm not saying he'd go so far as to try to kill you, but it would be very convenient for him if you were to have some sort of accident or get sick. There's only three weeks to go until the bid is declared—anything that took you out of circulation now could tip the balance. And when you're standing out there on the pavement, looking up at what used to be your office, don't say I didn't warn you that he fights dirty.'

'Oh, I don't have time for this!' she snapped impatiently. 'The board meeting's due to start in ten minutes. Besides, I'm still not convinced that he really is behind Falcon—you haven't shown me a shred of solid proof. And even if he is, it doesn't make any sense— why should he be so desperate to get his hands on

Geldard's? We aren't in competition with him—in fact he's one of our suppliers. We buy a lot of sugar-cane from him, olives, sorghum...'

Jake perched himself on the side of her desk. 'Have you ever heard of a place called Nuevo Saltar?' he asked.

'Yes...' She frowned, flipping through her mental Filofax to recall the details. 'It's a peasant's co-operative in the Chacabuco area—we signed a contract with them about six months ago, to supply us with peanut-oil. But what's that got to do with it? It's a very small contract—insignificant compared to what we buy from Juan.'

'Insignificant to you, maybe, but not to Juan. Did you know he pays his farmhands virtual slave wages? They've had to put up with it because there's been no alternative—until that co-operative started up, practically on the doorstep of one of his biggest spreads. Suddenly the word is getting around among his workers that there could be a chance of a better life for them—they're starting to get restless, asking for higher pay. And he doesn't like it. In the bad old days, he could have sent in a few hired guns and shot the place up, but the government have made it more than clear that they're not prepared to tolerate that sort of thing so he's having to be a bit more subtle. If he could take you over he could dump the contract, and the co-operative would be in serious trouble.'

Georgia stared at him, shaking her head in bewilderment. 'I don't believe it... He'd go to all the trouble of taking over Geldard's just to stamp out a tiny little operation like that?'

He nodded grimly. 'It may be tiny, but to de Perez it's like a mosquito—irritating and potentially dangerous. And it's a machismo thing—he has to show that he's the boss. Of course, there are other gains to be had. The world's becoming a tough place to trade—Geldard's is a well-established company, a guaranteed market for

him. Not to mention a doorway into Europe. I think
he's weighed it all up very carefully.'

She slanted him a searching glance from beneath her
lashes. 'How do you know all this about him?' she
queried.

'I've made it my business to find out. I was involved
in a land deal a couple of years ago that went sour in a
very nasty way. The company that was behind it was
called Condor,' he added with a dry laugh. 'Not a very
big leap to your Falcon. I found out that there'd been
a number of similar unpleasant incidents, causing a lot
of damage to honest people. So I started doing a little
amateur investigating—I've got pretty extensive con-
tacts and I can find out a lot of information that other
people wouldn't have a chance of getting their hands on.
The trail eventually led me to the Bahamas, but then it
got lost in a labyrinth of holding companies, sheltering
under their banking secrecy laws. There was just one
clue—which pointed in the general direction of de Perez's
son, César; I was following him to Bermuda, but unfortunately he'd left just before I arrived.'

Georgia almost choked. Damn—why hadn't she made
the connection before? If Jake was right, that explained
why César had been so keen to marry her—his father
had probably been putting pressure on him to persuade
her to marry him as a means of gaining control of the
company.

Juan wouldn't have been too pleased with the boy for
making such a hash of it, she reflected wryly—though
it was probably his own fault for driving him to such
dramatic extremes. And then he had decided to try se-
ducing her himself—to persuade her to be his mistress,
to run away with him to a tropical island. The rat...!

Jake was regarding her with shrewd curiosity. 'Do you
know something else?' he enquired.

'No!' She felt her cheeks flush a heated red. 'All right—I'll…have a bodyguard, if you really think I need one. Satisfied?'

He nodded, the glint in his eyes warning her that the matter wasn't completely settled. 'Satisfied,' he conceded.

'Well? It's been two weeks, and no one's tried to poison me, or run my car off the road, or drop a piano out of a window onto my head. Your precious bodyguards have been a complete waste of time.'

Jake shrugged his wide shoulders in that characteristic gesture of unconcern. 'Maybe it's because they're there that no one's tried to drop a piano on your head,' he responded in that lazy, mocking drawl.

'And would you mind taking your feet off my desk?' Georgia demanded irritably. She was too hot—even the modern, expensive air-conditioning plant in the Geldard building was having difficulty coping with the soaring August temperatures—and she was tired. With the clock ticking inexorably away on the takeover bid, she had been working twenty hours a day, almost obsessively checking and double-checking every detail. The last thing she needed was Jake Morgan hanging around, cluttering up her tidy office, unsettling her.

He laughed, making no attempt to move the offending size twelves, clad in a pair of scuffed desert boots that belied the healthy state of his bank balance. 'Loosen up, Blondie,' he taunted. 'You've been working your butt off, but now Falcon have made their final offer all you can do is sit back and wait for the result to be called. So why not do what everyone else is doing? Enjoy the Bank Holiday.'

Georgia slanted him a withering look. 'What about your own business?' she enquired. 'Doesn't that need any of your attention?'

'Nothing I can't deal with by phone or fax. The wonders of modern technology, you see—it brings the whole world to your doorstep.'

'How wonderfully convenient,' she retorted acidly.

'Isn't it just? So how about it? We have three whole days—why don't we go off somewhere? I hear the Lake District is a pretty spot—or Scotland, maybe? I've never been to Scotland. You could show me the sights.'

'No, thank you.'

'All right—how about dinner and then the theatre? There's a couple of really good things on I wouldn't mind seeing.'

Georgia sighed through her teeth, shaking her head.

He chuckled with laughter. 'So I suppose a weekend of mad, passionate lovemaking is out of the question?' he taunted provocatively.

She refused to permit herself to smile, though it was a struggle. Leaning across her desk, she flicked the switch on the intercom. 'Hello, Donald? I'll be leaving in a few moments—I'll meet you down in the car park, as usual.'

'Yes, Miss Geldard.'

Jake was frowning. 'Donald?' he queried sharply. 'That's not your usual chauffeur—where's Maurice?'

'On holiday,' she responded with strained patience. 'This one's from the pool. And he's been fully vetted.'

'So I should hope,' he countered. 'Even so, I think I'll ride home with you—just in case.'

'In case of what? All our pool drivers have done the defensive driving course, and there'll be sixteen stone of hired muscle in the seat beside him. Oh, but maybe an elephant will escape from Regent's Park Zoo and charge the car. Or an asteroid will fall from the sky and knock me unconscious, whereupon I'll be rushed to hospital, where there'll be a dreadful mix-up and they'll amputate my leg by mistake!'

His eyes glinted in appreciative humour. 'Maybe not, but you can't be too careful,' he insisted. 'Come on, how bad can it be? Half an hour? Say three-quarters, allowing for the holiday traffic. You can put up with my company for that long, surely?'

Georgia didn't deign to respond—partly because she didn't care to admit just how much of a strain it would be. It had been a difficult and lonely time, these past few weeks, struggling to hold onto her birthright, not knowing who she could trust. At times it would have been so easy to pretend that she really did believe that she was in danger, to let herself sink into the shelter of those strong arms... But fortunately, whenever she'd come too dangerously close to succumbing to that treacherous temptation, she'd had only to recall that iniquitous bet.

With a last swift glance around the office to check that everything was safely locked away, she headed for the lift. Though it was barely six o'clock, the building was virtually deserted—even the most dedicated workaholics had left on time to make the most of the Bank Holiday weekend. And it looked like being a sizzler— the long heatwave showed no sign of breaking, though the weather report had promised a thunderstorm within the next few days.

'Do you have any plans for the weekend?' she enquired in a sardonically polite tone as the lift arrived and Jake stepped into it with her.

'Not a great deal—if I can't persuade you to spend it with me,' he responded, putting on a wistful air belied by the gleam of wickedness in those deep-set hazel eyes.

'Oh?' She pressed the button for the basement car park. 'Not seeing your supermodel any more?'

He laughed, shaking his head. 'I haven't been out with her for months. I've never been celibate for such a long time—I'm sure it's not good for my health.'

This time Georgia couldn't suppress the smile that curved her soft mouth—she didn't believe a word of it, but it was amusing nevertheless. 'Nonsense,' she retorted crisply. 'It won't do you the least harm.'

'Ah, I knew you were cruel,' he teased, leaning both hands against the lift wall on each side of her shoulders. 'How can you watch me suffer like this, when one kiss from those sweet, tender lips would ease my pain...?'

His mouth was just inches from hers, his breath warm against her cheek... And deep inside her a melting pang of need was undermining all her carefully constructed defences... But at that moment the lift reached the basement, coming to a halt with a slight bump, and as the doors slid open she smiled up at him with mingled triumph and regret, ducking beneath his arm and stepping out into the car park.

She had gone three paces when she sensed something was wrong; there was no sign of the ice-blue Rolls Royce. As she hesitated a movement in the shadows caught her eye, and she half turned... too late to warn Jake as he stepped out of the lift and straight under the fall of a heavy cosh.

As his large frame crumpled to the ground at her feet she screamed—a scream that was swiftly muffled by a rough hand over her mouth.

'Shut her up!' a harsh voice ordered. There were three of them, all wearing balaclavas over their faces. 'Come on, get her into the van.'

'What about 'im?' one of the others asked.

'He'll have to come along too. Make sure you tie 'im up good—I don't fancy tangling with 'im when 'e wakes up. And I don't want to hear a peep out of neither of 'em, neither.'

Georgia had recovered from the initial shock sufficiently to begin to struggle, but it quickly became more than apparent that she had no chance of escaping—her hands and feet were tied and a thick cloth wrapped around her mouth, so that she could do no more than squeak indignantly as she was bundled without ceremony into the back of an old transit van, landing on top of a heap of old rags. Jake, similarly bound and gagged, was thrown in beside her, and the doors slammed shut, leaving her in total darkness.

The van jolted sharply, throwing her against his long, hard body, and instinctively she nestled against it—partly for comfort and partly for the reassurance of feeling him still breathing. He had been right all along, she realised in growing horror—and she had been too damned stupid and obstinate to believe him.

It was still difficult to believe that Juan could do anything this evil. She hadn't seen him since that disastrous weekend in Cowes, and had assumed that he had gone back to Argentina. But then ... maybe it wasn't so difficult to believe, after all—if a man had so little regard for his marriage vows, why should she expect him to have any more regard for anything else?

And what was going to happen now? Perhaps she should have tried to remember the turns the van had made, so that she would have some idea of where they were being taken, but it had already speeded up on what was clearly a long, wide stretch of road, and she had an uncomfortable suspicion that they were heading out of London altogether.

To her relief, Jake began to stir—he must have been unconscious for almost ten minutes. She lifted her head to try to see his face—her eyes had grown a little more accustomed to the darkness now—and she could just make out his hard-drawn features. He groaned, and then suddenly jerked against his bonds as he realised that he was tied up. Then, sensing her beside him, he levered himself up on one elbow to look down at her—and even in the darkness she could read the kaleidoscope of emotions reflected in his eyes.

She could respond only with her own eyes, trying to convey a wry apology—for not believing him and for putting him in this kind of danger. She hadn't seen a gun, but she wouldn't be at all surprised if their abductors were armed—and her fear was that they wouldn't hesitate to shoot him if they thought it necessary.

It seemed that he must have come to a similar conclusion; she recognised the moment of which his instinctive response of explosive anger gave way to a bitter realisation of the need for a more careful strategy. He lay back against the bundles of rags, frowning as he considered the options.

It was clear that normal channels of communication were impossible, to suggest they turn back-to-back and try to unpick each other's knots. Georgia could only nudge him and turn over herself. He took up her message at once, manoeuvring himself around close behind her, his fingers probing the soft nylon cord that bound her wrists.

He didn't seem to be having much success; the stuff had been well-chosen, the knots bedding in on themselves so that even if he had been able to see what he was doing it would have been well-nigh impossible to unfasten them. Lying awkwardly back-to-back, in a fast-moving vehicle that was jolting them around most uncomfortably, it was an exercise in total frustration.

She had no better luck, though her fingers were smaller and more nimble than his. Even when they tried both sitting up, leaning back against each other with their feet braced against the side of the van in an attempt to hold themselves steady, they were still rocked round far too much to be able to work on one thread consistently, and though she broke several of her well manicured nails she seemed to be making no impression on the knots at all.

Jake grunted, losing patience. Swinging himself around, he kicked out violently with his feet against the door of the van—as much, it seemed, out of a need to release his pent-up rage as in any hope that it would give way. The only effect was that the small hatch from the driver's compartment was slid open, and the rough voice of the one who appeared to be the leader of the gang growled, 'Oi—the pair of you. Shut up, right?'

Like a bull provoked by a red rag, Jake kicked out again, battering at the unyielding door—though the heat in his eyes should have been enough to burn through the metal like a laser. The response from the front was everything Georgia had feared, the sinister muzzle of a gun appeared, grey in the fading afternoon light filtering into their mobile prison.

'Shut up, I said,' the voice grated. 'Lie down and don't move.'

To Georgia's relief, Jake appeared to decide that discretion, under such uneven circumstances, was the better part of valour. He lay back on the rags again, outwardly acquiescent, but the narrowed slits of his eyes warned that the first chance he got to turn the tables would make their assailants rue the day they had been born.

After a few moments the gun was withdrawn and the hatch closed, leaving them in darkness once more. Georgia edged herself around so that she could sit with her back against the side of the van—she was beginning to feel cramped and the cord was rubbing against her wrists. Her mind kept playing back over the moment of their kidnap, wondering if there had been anything she could have done to avert it, though she knew it would be more productive to try to think ahead and plan some means of escape.

Of course, it would have been much easier for them by the fact that her usual chauffeur was on holiday— someone had probably intercepted her call to Donald and instructed him to meet her outside the front door instead. Maurice would have known that she never did that—in the narrow City streets, a large Rolls Royce waiting at the kerb could cause a major traffic obstruction within two minutes.

And that same someone must have helped the kidnappers get into the secure underground car park—which meant that there was someone on the inside of her organisation who had betrayed her, she reflected with an uncomfortable pang. It was horrible to think that someone close to her could have done a thing like that.

Who? Janet? Bernard? One of her domestic staff? No—she was sure she could trust all of them. The most likely candidate was one of her uncles—maybe even both of them. That was the thanks her grandfather got for bringing them both into the business, settling shares on them, she reflected bitterly.

Of course, she knew they resented the fact that she, a mere female, had cut them both out of succession—a resentment exceeded only by their bitter rivalry towards each other. If either of them had perceived in this takeover bid an opportunity to trounce both her and the other, he could easily have persuaded himself to ignore the consequences.

So what was the plan? To make her disappear for a few days with some sort of plausible cover story about how she had been under a lot of strain lately—a hint that she was on the verge of a nervous breakdown? And no doubt the details of how she had done a similar vanishing act in Bermuda would add even more credibility to the tale. By the time she showed up again, loudly protesting foul play, she'd have a difficult job persuading anyone to believe her—and Juan would have the company safely in his pocket. Damn, damn, damn!

It was uncomfortably hot in the van, and she was beginning to get thirsty. How much longer was this nightmare drive going to take? She could guess from their speed that they were on a motorway, but which one? Heading north, towards Yorkshire or Scotland, or south—towards the Channel Tunnel? Surely they wouldn't risk trying to smuggle them through there, where they might be stopped by Customs?

North then, most probably—there were plenty of bleak and lonely places up there, where they could be hidden for as long as necessary. Actually they wouldn't have to hold them for very long; as soon as the news of her "breakdown" got around, there would be a panic of selling—and once Falcon had fifty-one percent of the shares they could let them go.

Of course they would let them go—her mind refused to consider the possibility that they might not. Even Juan wouldn't dare have them killed...

She shifted her position, trying to ease the discomfort of her bonds. Jake seemed to have gone to sleep—she could hear his slow, deep breathing, see the dark hump of his body stretched out on the floor of the van. How on earth could he sleep, under these circumstances? Did he have nerves of steel? Maybe she ought to try to do the same, she reflected wryly—after all, there wasn't a lot else she could do.

Swinging herself around, she lay down beside him, letting her head rest against his arm. If only she had believed him; he had been trying to protect her and she wouldn't listen. He had told her once to start listening to her instincts—but how could she do that, when she had been taught all her life to be afraid of them? She didn't know how to begin.

Maybe in her dreams... There her senses ruled, un-fettered by the rigid controls of her conscious mind; there she was free to surrender to the sweet temptation, caught in the mesmerising spell of those deep-set, hazel eyes.

Sleep came, however unlikely it had seemed—a sleep of sheer mental exhaustion, lulled by the gentle rocking motion of the speeding van; it was a sleep that replaced the nightmare of reality with a world of beguiling possibilities, a world where anything could happen...

CHAPTER EIGHT

GEORGIA was jolted abruptly awake, her shock at finding herself tied hand and foot resolving swiftly into a terrifying recollection of what had happened. The van had stopped, and the back door was being unlocked. Beside her, Jake had woken and sat up; in the darkness, the look he slanted her was calm and reassuring—somehow, in spite of everything, she sensed that while he was with her there was nothing to be afraid of.

There seemed to be some sort of discussion going on outside, to the effect that their feet were going to have to be untied, but any hope she might have had that they could make a run for it was dashed when the door swung open and she found herself confronted by the gun again—pointing not at her, but at Jake.

'OK, move,' she was ordered gruffly, as one of the gang dragged her out of the van and shoved her towards a single-storey prefabricated building.

She had a fleeting moment to glance around; it was an eerie scene, lit only by moonlight. Above her, all around, rose sheer walls of scarred rock; she was in a flat-bottomed pit, littered with heaps of slag and rusting machinery—a disused quarry, worked out and long forgotten. The only sound was the steady chug of a petrol generator, echoing off the barren cliffs; they could have been on another planet.

A rough hand in the small of her back urged her up a step into the building. It appeared to have been used as the quarry office at one time—there was a desk and a battered grey filing cabinet, and several old notices tacked to a board on the wall. The walls had been painted an unpleasant mustard-coloured gloss and the floor was covered with worn lino—and there were wire grilles over all the windows.

Her captor pushed her along a dark, narrow passage and into a small, square room. Jake was pushed in behind her, and then the rope around her wrists was cut before the door was closed with an ominous thud and she heard several bolts being shot across.

With a sigh of relief she unfastened the gag across her mouth and took stock of her surroundings. The room was about nine feet square. The windows were boarded up, and the only furniture was an old wooden bed and a table and chair. It might have looked a little better if it hadn't been so brightly lit, she reflected ruefully—after the darkness she had become accustomed to for the past few hours, the glare made her eyes sting.

The sound of a muffled grunt pointedly drew her attention to the fact that Jake was still tied up. 'Oh, I'm sorry...' She bent to examine the soft cord knotted around his wrists. It had been tied rather tighter than hers, and was cutting quite badly into his skin—she felt a sharp stab of pain at the realisation that it must be hurting him. 'Oh, dear, it's going to take me ages to untangle this.'

She unfastened the gag first, and he drew in a deep gasp of air, shaking his head. 'Thank goodness for that!' His eyes slanted her a mocking look. 'Bodyguards were a waste of time, huh? Looks like you were talking a bit too soon.'

'I know,' she conceded wryly. 'Go on, you can say "I told you so" if it makes you feel any better.'

'What would make me feel better at the moment would be getting that damned cord off my wrists. Can't you work any faster?'

'It's very tricky stuff—no wonder we couldn't get it off in the van... Ah, that's it, it's coming...' At last the knots began to yield to her intricate unpicking, unravelling slowly until the cord fell away—she couldn't help but notice his slight wince of pain as he examined the scarlet weals. He had a bump on his forehead, too, where he had been hit with the cosh. 'Are you all right?' she asked with concern.

'I'll live,' he responded, an inflection of sardonic humour in his voice. He glanced around the room. 'Not exactly the Ritz, is it? And it looks as though they were only expecting to provide accommodation for one.'

'What do you think will happen when they realise who you are?' she queried anxiously.

Those hazel eyes glinted darkly. 'That's an interesting question,' he conceded.

And one to which she didn't really want to know the answer, Georgia reflected as she sat down despondently on the bed. A glance at her watch told her that it was almost two o'clock in the morning, but the room was still uncomfortably hot and stuffy—the sun would have been beating down on the flat roof all day, turning it to an oven.

Jake was prowling around, exploring; there was a door in one corner and he laughed aloud as he opened it. 'Ah—this appears to be the executive washroom.'

'Oh, big deal,' Georgia retorted on a burst of impatience. 'I'm delighted to hear it.'

'You will be in a little while,' he predicted grimly.

He was right, of course—though that made it no better. He was always right, damn him. She watched him now as he carefully quartered the room, minutely examining every detail of the walls, the boarded-up windows, even the floor—lifting the lino to check the boards beneath. Finally he began to examine the ceiling, fetching the chair to stand on and running his fingers around the joints and screws holding the cheap plaster-board in place. Just inside the washroom, he seemed to find what he wanted.

'What have you got in your handbag?' he asked.

'In my handbag?' With some astonishment, she realised that it was on the floor by the door; their captors must have picked it up after she had dropped it when the first one had grabbed her, back in the basement car park beneath the Geldard building—to leave it behind would have been a damning clue. 'Not a lot—my keys, some credit cards, a little money...'

'A nail file?'

'Yes, I think so...'

'Good. Get it for me, then go and stand by the door and listen, and warn me if anyone's coming.'

The bag had been rifled though, and to her fury she found that the small amount of cash she carried had been stolen. 'Of all the petty...! There couldn't have been more than about twenty pounds in it!' she protested.

'Never mind that now,' Jake responded crisply. 'The nail file?'

She found it in her make-up purse, and handed it up to him. 'If you're going to try and dig your way out with that, we could be here till Christmas,' she remarked, trying not to let fear creep into her voice.

'It could take a while,' he conceded. 'But not as long as that. Keep your ear to the door.'

There was something reassuring in his confidence, in his presence. Somehow, in spite of everything, she couldn't help feeling that he would succeed in getting them safely out of here—he just wasn't the type to let himself be caged up like this, or to let anyone get the better of him.

Watching him as he worked on the screws, patiently scraping away the layers of paint that glued them in place, she realised that she ought to be able to let herself trust him. He had been protecting her even when she had been too obstinate to see that she was at risk—and she was quite sure that it was he who had arranged the business crisis, and the punch-up, that had prevented her from having to face the consequences of her own folly in going away with Juan for the weekend.

And surely he wouldn't have gone to all that trouble if he didn't feel anything for her? The question was a dangerous one, luring her into building dreams that could still prove to be founded on nothing but sand. After all, there was still the small matter of that iniquitous bet...

A sound on the other side of the door, a foot-fall, brought her suddenly alert, and she tapped Jake's knee, her eyes expressing a silent warning. Like a cat, moving swiftly and without a sound, he was down from the chair, swinging it back into place and sitting on it, his arms resting on the table as if he had been there for the past hour.

The bolts were slid back and the door opened a couple of inches—but it was held in place by two thick chains. 'Don't try anything—I've still got the gun,' a gruff voice warned.

'Stand over there by the wall, where I can see you.' They moved into place, observed by one beady eye still peering through the hole in a balaclava. 'OK. Here's summat to eat.' A hand reached cautiously through the gap and placed a brown paper bag on the floor.

'Have you got a pack of cards?' Jake demanded testily. 'It's pretty damned boring sitting here with nothing to do.'

There was a crude chuckle. 'Blimey, nothing to do? Banged up with a tasty piece of crackling like that? I'd have plenty to do. All right, I'll see if I can find you a spare pack. Anything else you'd like?' he added on a note of acid sarcasm.

'A beer would go down well,' Jake responded, ever hopeful.

'Yeah, wouldn't it just? Well, I can't have none, so you can't have none neither. Just think yerself lucky you've got this much—you could have got nothing.'

As the door slammed shut Jake pulled a wry face. 'I suppose that's right,' he acknowledged, strolling over to fetch the food bag. 'At least it proves they're not planning to kill us—at least not yet.'

'You think they might ?' she queried anxiously.

He didn't answer, simply shrugging his wide shoulders in an eloquent gesture and turning his attention to the contents of the brown paper bag. 'Let's see—what have we got in here? Sandwiches—looks like one round of ham and tomato, and one of cheese and tomato. A couple of apple pies... Correction—apple and blackcurrant. And a couple of cans of cola.' He unpacked each item onto the table. 'What do you fancy?'

'I don't fancy anything,' she retorted crossly. 'How can you possibly eat at a time like this?'

'We have to keep our strength up—once we get out of here, we could have a helluva hike to get back to civilisation. You can't do that on an empty stomach.' He unwrapped a pack of the sandwiches and handed one to her. 'Eat,' he ordered.

She glared at him in angry defiance, and then snatched the sandwich from him, biting into it viciously. 'Do you always have to be right?' she demanded.

'No—just most of the time.' There was a glint of mocking humour in those intriguing hazel eyes. 'I hope I'm right about you.'

'Oh?' She arched one finely drawn eyebrow.

'That you've got the guts to get out of here,' he responded grimly. 'That you won't go throwing hysterics on me.'

'Of course I've got the guts!' she retorted, her anger flaring. 'I'd just like to know how you think you're going to do it.'

'Through the roof,' he explained patiently, as if to a small child.

'You don't think maybe they might hear you?' she queried.

'I'm working on that one.'

'Good. When you come up with an idea—a sensible one—just let me know.'

'What an ungrateful wench you are, Blondie,' he taunted. 'I hope, when all this is over, you'll thank me properly.'

There was no mistaking what he meant by that. 'I am *not* a wench,' she raged, scarlet flaring her cheeks. 'And don't call me Blondie!'

He laughed softly, huskily, and leaning over the table brushed her lips lightly with his own. 'You're so beautiful when you're angry,' he mocked lightly, and, downing a long swig of cola from the can, he picked up the chair and returned to his task.

'Oh-h! Can it get any *hotter* in here?' Georgia asked wearily, dabbing her forehead and the back of her neck with a damp tissue. 'I'm beginning to think I'll go crazy if we're stuck in here much longer. I thought you said you were going to get us out?'

'Patience,' Jake chided her. 'It's just taking a little longer than I thought.'

'Maybe you're not really trying,' she countered. 'Maybe you're just pretending, to keep me quiet. Maybe you *are* the one behind all this, after all.'

'If I'm trying to keep you quiet, I'm not making a very good job of it, am I?' he retorted drily. 'And you think I arranged to have myself knocked on the head? Very clever of me, that.'

'Well, you could have done—to add a bit of realism,' she argued. 'How do I know?'

He paused for a moment in what he was doing, leaning his hands against the top of the doorframe and ducking his head beneath it to look down at her with mocking amusement. 'Frankly, if I'd arranged this myself, I'd be battering on the door to be let out by now,' he remarked cordially. 'Twenty-four hours locked up with you would be enough to drive any man out of his skull.'

'Until yesterday, you were expecting me to believe you wanted nothing more than to spend the night with me,' she pointed out.

'I didn't have in mind a two-foot-wide bed with a mattress made of steel wool, and a woman who expected me to sleep top-to-tail with my damned jeans on!'

'I felt safer that way!'

'You seriously think I'd have tried making love to you with those thick-headed gorillas who kidnapped us listening at the door?'

'Well . . . why not?' she protested, her cheeks flaming scarlet. 'I don't see why that would have stopped you.'

His mouth curved into a wicked grin. 'I was afraid you might get a bit too enthusiastic,' he taunted. 'I'll bet you're the sort of woman who makes a lot of noise.' And before she could think of a suitable retort his head had disappeared as he turned his attention back to the washroom ceiling.

Georgia slid down to the floor, resting her back against the door as she continued to listen for any warning sound of approach on the other side. It was now late Saturday evening—they had been locked in here for a whole night and day, and it was looking as if they'd be here for considerably longer. It was stiflingly hot, adding to the sense of claustrophobia created by the four dun-coloured walls around them.

'We could do with a storm—a really good thunder-storm. That would clear the air.'

'Uh-huh.'

She tipped her head back to look up at him. From this angle that big, powerful frame looked more impressive than ever: long legs in casual denim that interestingly moulded a neat, masculine behind, a taut, muscular mid-section beneath the cling of a white T-shirt, and shoulders as wide as a cliff...

She had never been quite so physically aware of a man before, but there was no mistaking the flutter of tension in the pit of her stomach every time she was near him. In spite of all her prim insistence last night that he keep his clothes on and sleep with his head at the other end of the bed to hers, she had been aching to lie in his strong arms, to feel those big, sensitive hands caressing her, to feel the weight of his body on hers...

Struggling to keep control of her sanity, she shook the dangerous thoughts from her brain, drawing in a slow, deep breath to steady the erratic beating of her heart. 'You know, I don't really know very much about you,' she remarked, hoping to get the conversation back onto a more even keel. 'Where you come from, how you got started...'

He ducked his head below the doorframe again, regarding her with cynical amusement. 'You think I sprang up with the last crop of mushrooms?' he queried. 'You've had me investigated—didn't you read the file?'

Her cheeks flamed a guilty red. 'All right, so I did,' she conceded. 'But it was only the bare bones...when you were born, where you went to school, your employment record. It didn't really tell me much about *you*.'

He had returned to his task of breaking up the insulation layer in the roof, and for a moment she thought he wasn't going to answer. 'All right,' he said at last. 'Well, you'll know that I was born in a place called Port

Macquarie, which is maybe a hundred miles north of
Sydney. My father could have been any one of half a
dozen guys—my mother could never be sure. She died
when I was twelve, and me and my kid brother were sent
to a foster-home, on a sheep station on the Willandra
River. It was a pretty good place to grow up—my brother
still lives there, helping our foster-parents work the
station.'

'But…you decided to leave?' she prompted carefully.

'I got an offer from my grandfather to go and work
for him in Sydney.' His voice had taken on a hard edge.
'He hadn't been planning on it—he'd have preferred to
forget I even existed. But unfortunately for him his son
and grandson had been killed in a car crash, leaving him
without another heir. So he decided he'd better take a
look at me, see if I measured up.'

'And…did you?' Georgia queried, holding her breath.

'I took one look at him and didn't want to. He was
a mean, puritanical old hypocrite—kept his secretary as
his mistress but condemned my mother for the life she'd
led, the life he'd driven her to. But I stayed for three
and a half years—long enough to learn what I needed
to about the construction business. Then I left, and got
myself a job on an oil-rig in Saudi for a couple of years
while I saved up enough money to get a start.

'When I got back to Australia, I went to Perth. It was
really buzzing there then—millionaires springing up all
over the place. I started out building swimming-pools,
and it just went on from there. And then, when I was
big enough, I moved back to Sydney.' Now there was
an unmistakable note of menace in his voice.

'It took me five years to destroy my grandfather's
business. After he'd gone bankrupt, I bought up the
company for a song—I've never laughed so much as the
day he was forced to sign the papers that made it mine.
I had an old photograph of my mother, with me on her

lap as a baby—she'd only have been about eighteen or nineteen. I'd had it put in a big silver frame, and I stuck it right there on what had been his desk. I thought he was going to be sick.'

Georgia felt a small chill feather down her spine. She could understand why he had done what he had, but his single-minded pursuit of such conclusive revenge was further proof—if she had needed it—of his ruthlessness. He would make a very dangerous enemy.

'So that's it,' he concluded. 'The rest, no doubt, you have on record. Now, let me ask you something. You know something about what César was doing in Bermuda—what is it?'

She hesitated, reluctant to admit how foolish she had been. 'I...don't know exactly what he was doing there— I only went aboard his boat once, and that...wasn't exactly voluntary.'

'Oh?'

'He kidnapped me,' she admitted wryly. 'I was escaping from him when I...ran into you.'

He swung on the frame of the door and dropped to the ground, crouching down beside her. 'You don't say?' he mused. 'Well, now, that's...very interesting. Why did he kidnap you?'

'He said he...wanted to marry me.' She shook her head impatiently. 'Of course I suspected all along that there was something else to it. Obviously he and his father were already scheming to gain control of Geldard's.'

Jake shook his head. 'Not necessarily the two of them together,' he mused pensively. 'I think César may have been trying to get one jump ahead of his father. There's no love lost between them—César has always taken his mother's side, though unfortunately he's learned too well his father's underhand methods of doing business. It's a pity; he's a bright lad. Shame you didn't take it as a warning, though,' he added, a sardonic inflection in his voice. 'I might have had less of a tough time convincing you to be careful of your own safety.'

'All right, so you were right about that too,' she conceded. 'But I just... I didn't know if I could trust you either. I still don't...'

That fascinating mouth curved into a smile that held no trace of his customary mockery. 'There's nothing I can say to you to make you believe in me,' he murmured softly. 'Just listen to your instincts.'

Without her even being aware of it, those hazel eyes had captured her in their spell, and she found herself drowning in their depths, her breathing ragged, her heartbeat accelerating out of control. He had asked her before to listen to her instincts... and she could feel her resistance beginning to waver.

But it was too much to ask—more than she knew how to give. She had only just begun to concede the possibility that perhaps his interest in her wasn't solely in order to gain control of Geldard's, that maybe he really *was* genuinely attracted to her after all... Except that there was the tiny matter of that bet still outstanding, she reminded herself bitterly—that ought to be enough to arm her against his practised seduction.

The sound of one of the bolts being drawn back brought them both abruptly to their feet, and by the time that disembodied hand appeared with their bag of sandwiches and cola they were both innocently on the other side of the room.

Georgia lay awake in the darkness, staring up at the yellow ceiling, listening to the slow, even sound of Jake breathing in his sleep. His feet were tucked against her shoulders, her feet beneath his arm, and she could feel the strong, hard-muscled length of his body against hers.

How could he sleep? It was such a sultry night, and with her clothes on she was much too hot. There was certainly going to be a thunderstorm—and the sooner the better. It was bad enough being cooped up in this horrible little room, not knowing what was going to happen—the tension was winding up her nerves until it felt as if they were going to snap.

Jake had managed to loosen one of the ceiling boards, but then there had been the long and tricky job of stripping away the roof lining. Anxious that the routine of opening the door only on the chain might change at any time, they had been obliged to conceal the stuff beneath the mattress, making it even more lumpy and uncomfortable to lie on.

Now he was through to the roof itself—thick plywood, overlaid with bitumen to make it waterproof. It had taken him hours to make a tiny hole with her nail file, just enough to get a few fingers into. And every time there was a noise close to the door he had had to stop, and wedge the ceiling board back in place in case one of their captors came in and looked around.

He was a pretty remarkable man, she mused, nestling herself a little more closely against him. She could only admire the steady determination that had kept him at his tedious task through the long, hot hours of the day. And she hadn't been the best of companions; the heat, the confinement, the all-pervading anxiety, had made her snappy at times, but he had been very patient with her.

She could almost imagine herself falling in love with him... Almost. But if she was ever going to let herself take the risk of falling in love, it would have to be with a man who might love her back—not one who only wanted to get her into bed to win a bet. Angry tears stung the backs of her eyes, and she blinked them back as she eased herself away from him.

Dammit, why had she ever met him? What laughing gods had decided to send his yacht across her path at just that moment? She had been happy before that—in her own way. At least she had known clearly what she wanted out of life. Now she was a prey to emotions she had always despised, the kind of emotions that made women weak and foolish—just like her mother...

Closing her eyes, she made an effort to clear her mind, to listen only to the sound of her own breathing as she willed herself to fall asleep. The problem was, once she did, her dreams would be waiting for her...

'God, I'm sick of being stuck in these clothes. What I wouldn't give for a nice cool shower, and the chance to slip into something clean.'

The only response was a grunt. It was late in the evening, and Jake had been working on the roof all day, breaking it away piece by piece with his bare hands. She knew she shouldn't be complaining about her own ills— his fingers were torn and bleeding, but he had paused only to run them under the cold tap for a few minutes before going back to work.

'How's it going?' she asked, leaning over and craning her head to peer up at the washroom ceiling. It was wonderful to see that chink of star-lit sky, proving that there was a real world still outside after all—she had begun to feel as though she would never see it again.

'Just a bit more.' He paused for a moment, breathing deeply. 'I think we could finally be in for that storm— there's a helluva black cloud up over there.'

'Well, that'll be a relief anyway.'

She leaned back against the door, closing her eyes with a sigh. The heat had been building up unbearably all day, to the point where it was almost difficult to breathe. Images of diving into a nice, cool swimming-pool had been torturing her mind—or of lying on sweet green grass, fresh with the morning dew...

She only hoped that Jake would manage to get them out of here while there was still time for her to put a spoke in Juan's plans. Every time she thought about the things he had done anger simmered inside her—the way he had tried to lure her into an affair, the way he had sneakily persuaded her to talk over her tactics with him, while appearing to be bored by the whole business...

It wouldn't be easy, though—there were at least two, possibly three men outside, and they were armed. And even if they were able to escape undetected, they were miles from anywhere, with no idea where they were. But somehow she was sure that Jake would succeed—there was something about him that made her feel as though he could do anything he set his mind to...

An almighty clap of thunder pealed over her head. 'Lord, that was close—' Before she had finished speaking there was another clap, louder than the first, making her catch her breath in shock.

'It's right above us,' Jake said. 'I think it might be...'

They didn't even hear the third thunderclap—it was drowned by the sound of an explosion near at hand—and at the same moment the lights went out, plunging the room into pitch-darkness. Georgia screamed, barely having time to register that the petrol generator that provided the electricity for the lights must have been struck when she realised that Jake had taken advantage of the noise to smash a hole in the roof big enough to get through, and was levering himself out.

'Stay there!' he hissed urgently, and disappeared.

Her heart turned over; surely he wasn't going to try to tackle them single-handed? True, he would have the element of surprise on his side, but only for the first split second. After that...

Through the door, she could hear the sounds of a scuffle—someone yelled, a shot was fired—followed by a horrible moment of silence. Then she heard the bolts being drawn back, and held her breath. A tall, familiar figure appeared in the doorway, silhouetted against the faint red flicker of the burning petrol generator beyond the far window.

'OK, Blondie—let's tie these two geeks up, then we can get out of here.'

'Jake!' On a surge of pure relief she threw herself across the room and into his arms, clinging to him as if she would never let him go.

'It's OK—you're safe, you're free,' he soothed, stroking her hair. 'It's all over.'

Tears were streaming down her face as her mouth sought urgently for his, her lips parting hungrily to welcome the sweet, sensuous swirl of his tongue. For one all too brief moment he held her, and kissed her, but then, taking her gently by the shoulders, he put her away from him.

'Unfortunately we don't have time for that now,' he murmured, a teasing inflection in his voice. 'We'd better tie these two up before they come round.'

'I...heard the gun go off?' she queried, anxiety wavering in her voice.

He grinned down at her reassuringly. 'Missed by a mile. Here, put it in your handbag—I've taken the clip out, but I don't want to leave it behind for them. Careful you don't smudge the fingerprints on it.'

Georgia regarded the weapon with distaste, but did as he suggested—the gun, after all, was evidence. In the outer room, one body was sprawled across the floor, out cold, and the other was groaning, shaking his head foggily as he levered himself up by the table. Before he properly had time to regather his senses Jake had tapped him, quite lightly, above the ear, and he slumped down again.

'Get that rope—we'd better tie this one up first.'

Georgia moved swiftly; they had left the rope they had untied from their own wrists on the floor under the bed, and she found it without too much difficulty in the dark. 'Where's the third one?' she asked anxiously.

'Not here. He seems to have taken the van—which means we're going to have to walk,' Jake responded as he expertly trussed up the first of the men. He was already coming round again, and was not best pleased to find the tables turned on him—his turn of phrase was colourful in the extreme.

Jake cuffed him warningly. 'Hey, watch your mouth— there's a lady present.' He finished off the knots, pulling the man down to sit on the chair. 'There—I hope you're as damned uncomfortable as I was.' The second man too was starting to stir, but Jake had him bound and in the other chair, facing his accomplice, before he had time to realise what was happening. 'Well, good evening, gentlemen,' he taunted them mockingly. 'Sorry we can't stay to enjoy any more of your generous hospitality. See you in court.'

It had started to rain, drumming on the roof of the hut like artillery fire. Georgia hesitated in the doorway, peering out. The lightning was still slicing through the sky, but now there was a fractional gap before the thunder came—the storm was moving away. The high cliff walls around them were half obscured by the driving sheets of rain, and the ground, parched for so long by the hot, arid summer, hissed and crackled like a cauldron as the huge, wet drops hit it; already puddles were forming, drifting with swirls of white steam.

'We're going to have to make a run for it,' Jake warned, close behind her. 'The other guy could come back any time, and even though we've got a gun I don't fancy having to use it if he's got one too.'

Georgia nodded. 'It's only a little drop of rain.' What did it matter if they got wet? She was free—and it was wonderful! Throwing wide her arms, she danced out into the rain. In seconds she was drenched, her hair plastered to her head, the thin silk of her blouse clinging almost transparently to the soft curves of her body. 'Oh, this is fabulous!' she cried, tipping up her face to welcome the sting of the heavy drops.

Jake laughed, catching her around the waist and swinging her round. 'Have I ever told you how gorgeous you look when you're soaking wet?' he teased.

'You're crazy!'

'*I'm* crazy? You're the one that's dancing!'

Suddenly she became serious again. 'We'd better hurry,' she urged anxiously, glancing around at the rain-sodden quarry pit. 'Which way should we go? We don't even know where we are.'

'We know we're where we don't want to be,' Jake returned, his eyes glinting with grim humour as he took her hand and led the way towards the start of a steep path that zigzagged up the rocky cliff. 'When we get to somewhere else, that's when we can stop and worry about it.'

CHAPTER NINE

IT FELT as if they had been walking for hours. The storm had moved on, but it was still raining, though a little less heavily than before. They had struck out away from the road, in case the third kidnapper should return, but it was hard work trudging over the bleak hills, bare and shelterless, the rough grass wet and slippery beneath their feet and only a few bedraggled-looking sheep to give any sign of life.

'Have you any idea which way we're going?' Georgia asked eventually.

'No more than you,' Jake conceded. 'I'm just trying to head downhill all the time—that way I figure we're sure to come to a road, or at least a river we can follow.'

Georgia sighed, and then sneezed. Jake slide a protective arm around her shoulders, drawing her close against the warmth of his body.

'You must be freezing,' he sympathised, with a gentle concern that almost compensated for the discomfort of her condition. 'Come on, keep going—maybe we'll find a cottage or something.'

'Or something,' she returned wryly. 'We'd be lucky to even see it in this.'

Tucked safely into the curve of his arm, she trudged on, trying to ignore the fact that her shoes—designed for elegance on city pavements, not hiking over muddy hills in the pouring rain—were soaking wet and rubbing her bare feet. She had no choice but to keep going, but she was beginning to think she had escaped from the kidnappers only to die of pneumonia.

In the end, they did almost miss the building in the dark—little more than a sheep-byre, its walls of rough grey gritstone blended so well into the bleak landscape that it seemed almost a natural part of it. It had one tiny shuttered window and a wooden door held by an iron latch—it wasn't even locked.

'Must be some kind of shepherd's hut,' Jake observed as they groped their way in. 'It's not much, but at least it's dry.'

To Georgia, as Jake found a storm-lamp and a box of matches and gave them a little light, it seemed like paradise. The walls were of bare stone, and so was the floor, and the roof was open-beamed. In one corner there was a wooden platform, with a straw palliasse on it and a couple of rough woollen blankets. And, most welcome of all, there was a woodstove, with a neatly chopped stack of firewood piled beside it.

'I'll see if I can get this going,' Jake suggested, bending to open the stove and peer inside. 'You'd better get out of those wet clothes.'

He spoke quite casually, and it was after all the common sense thing to do, but Georgia hesitated, watching his wide back as he laid the wood and some paper in the stove and lit it with a match, blowing on it gently to encourage the flame. But already her wet shirt felt clammy and uncomfortable—it would be best to take it off and get herself properly dry.

She kicked off her shoes and then slowly began to unfasten the buttons down the front of her shirt. Peeling it back from her shoulders, she hung it carefully over the back of a wooden chair—in the heat that was already coming from the stove, it would be dry very quickly. Then, with fingers that felt a little numb, she reached round to the clasp of her skirt, unclipping that, sliding down the zip and stepping carefully out of it—that too she arranged on the chair.

Jake must have known that she was taking her clothes off, but he didn't turn from the stove until the wood was burning merrily. Then he closed the door on it and glanced up at her over his shoulder. Standing there a little awkwardly, in nothing but a dainty bra and briefs of sheer white lace, the soft glow of the storm-lamp caressing her creamy-gold skin, Georgia felt the heat of his gaze sliding over her—and the unmistakable glint of approval she saw in those deep-set hazel eyes made her heart skip and begin to accelerate.

Slowly he rose to his feet, seeming even taller in the low-roofed byre—she had to tip her head back to look up at him. She felt as if she was rooted to the spot, and her mouth seemed to have gone strangely dry; they were alone now, in exactly the kind of circumstances in which she would have expected him to take advantage of her— and suddenly she was afraid that he wouldn't.

'You'd... better wrap yourself up in a blanket,' he suggested, his voice low and husky. He reached over to pick one up from the bed, never taking is eyes off her as he wrapped it carefully around her shoulders. And then, almost as if unable to help himself, he drew her into his arms, his eyes dark and smoky as they gazed down into hers.

For one long moment it seemed as though the whole world had paused, captured in a trance-like stillness; the only sounds were the crackling of the wood in the stove and the melancholy patter of rain on the roof. And then slowly he bent his head and kissed her, soft and intimate, his tongue gently exploring her mouth as if it was for the very first time.

Heat shivered through her as she curved herself against him. The blanket felt rough against her naked skin and she wanted to let it drop, to feel herself naked against the hard length of his body. The hunger that had been building inside her had become almost overwhelming;

she had never believed herself to be the kind of woman who would succumb to such basic, primitive instincts, but everything she had once been so sure of seemed to have been turned upside down.

She wanted him to make love to her, wanted him to slowly strip off the last remaining scraps of her underwear and caress her naked body with his strong, skilful hands, to tease the taut, tender nubs of her nipples until they stung with sweet pleasure, to ease apart her thighs and claim the submission of her body with his hard, penetrating thrusts...

As if he sensed her surrender in her response to his kiss, he lifted his head, a question in his eyes.

'Your clothes are wet too,' she whispered tensely. 'You...ought to take them off.'

'Yes, I...suppose I should...'

The light from the storm-lamp defined the hard lines of his face with shadow, and as he peeled the sopping T-shirt over his head it fell across the sculpted muscles in his wide chest, golden on his sun-bronzed skin. A single drop of rain fell from his wet hair and trailed slowly down through the light smattering of rough curls, and she watched its passage, mesmerised.

'And...your jeans?' she queried, her mouth dry.

'Yes.'

But he made no move to take them off, and so, with a boldness she would never have dreamed she possessed, she reached out her own hands and unbuckled the thick leather belt, took the tab of the zip between her fingers. Lifting her eyes briefly to his, she knew that he was waiting to see if she had the courage—there could be no doubting that once she had gone that far, there could be no turning back.

Her cheeks suffused with pink, she lowered her lashes and very carefully slid down the zip, trying not to let her trembling fingers brush against him. But as he kicked the wet denim away across the floor, he took her hand, laying it against his hair-roughened thigh.

'Touch me,' he whispered, his breath warm against her ear.

Tentatively, her hand trembling, she did. He was wearing silk-jersey boxer shorts, and through the smooth fabric she could feel the thick shaft of his manhood, hard as iron. With a small gasp she drew back, staring up at him, her eyes wide. But with the sureness of instinct she knew she could trust him not to hurt her. Holding open the blanket, she wrapped it with her arms around him, around them both, cocooning them in its warmth as their bodies met, naked flesh against naked flesh, her breasts in their taut lace cups brushing against the hard wall of his chest.

He laughed softly, low in his throat, brushing the wet strands of hair back from her face. 'The first time I met you, you looked like a drowned kitten,' he murmured. 'And now here you are—a drowned kitten again.'

A quivering smile curved her delicate mouth. No one had ever called her a kitten before—a cat, yes, when they had been on the receiving end of her sharp claws, but never a kitten. But he made her feel like a kitten— small and sensuous, rubbing her body invitingly against his. And only he knew just how to pet her to make her purr.

The glint in his dark eyes taunted her. 'Are you absolutely sure about this?' he queried. 'This time there's nowhere for you to disappear to but that cold, wet moor.'

'I'm sure,' she whispered, leaning up on tiptoe to brush her lips along the rough line of his jaw, where two days' growth of beard made his skin feel like coarse sandpaper. 'I want you to make love to me... Please.'

His arms folded around her, lifting her clean off her feet as his mouth claimed hers in a kiss that was almost savage in its intensity. For a fleeting moment her heart quickened in panic, as the ingrained fear of surrendering herself to her emotions rose up like a brick wall before her, but then she was crashing through it, swept away on the rising tide of her own urgent need, and she kissed him back, fiercely, hungrily, her tongue sparring with his and blissfully losing as he asserted the demand she had incited.

His hands were moving over her, exploring the curves and textures of her body, and her skin flamed beneath his touch, generating a heat that was melting her bones. Her head tipped back as she dragged raggedly for air, the walls of the hut swirling giddily around her as he spun her round and laid her down on the soft straw palliasse, still wrapped up in the blanket and his arms.

She hadn't even been aware that he had slipped off her bra, but as he lifted his head to gaze down at her she realised that her breasts were naked, firm and round, tipped with nipples as pink and inviting as ripe raspberries. She watched in a kind of fascination as his hands slid up over her smooth golden skin to cup and caress the aching fullness, his thumbs lightly teasing the tender nubs, so that she moaned softly, her spine arching as the sweet pleasure flooded through her.

'I've wanted to do this to you ever since that first time, when I dragged you out of the water and took you aboard my yacht, and you lay there on the couch like a lovely, naked nymph,' he growled huskily. 'I've wanted to stroke my hand over your warm, silken skin, to taste its honeyed sweetness, watch the spreading glow as it blushed with desire... I should have made love to you then,' he added on a note of wry self-mockery. 'Maybe, if I had, life would have been a lot simpler.'

An acute stab of pain sliced through her. Yes, life would have been simpler—for him at least. Having taken what he wanted, he would have been able to forget all about her, just as he no doubt forgot most of the women he made love to—except to remember as a pleasant interlude now and again. Instead, cheated of his prey, he had determined to have her, pursuing her with a ruthless intent—so confident of his ultimate success that he had even made a bet on it.

Well, he had won, she conceded, shamed by the willingness with which she had accepted her own defeat. With misted eyes she gazed down at his blond head as it bent over her naked breasts, his hot mouth dusting scalding kisses over their aching swell, the tip of his tongue tracing tantalising circles around the taut, sensitised peaks. In the end, her mind had proved to have no control over that treacherous female instinct, as old as Eve, to surrender to the physical supremacy of the male. And when he collected on his bet it would become public knowledge that she had finally succumbed.

But that knowledge was no defence against the onslaught of sensation that was shimmering through her, fueled by his expert caresses. With his hand he was keeping one breast at the peak of arousal, teasing and tugging at the tender nipple, rolling it beneath his palm, while the other he flicked with his hot tongue, reducing her to a state of helpless abandon as she stared up with unseeing eyes at the pattern of soft shadows cast by the golden glow of the storm-lamp against the wooden rafters above her head.

His mouth moved to the other breast, tormenting her with an exquisite anticipation as she felt the hot rasp of his tongue over the rawly sensitised nerve-ending of her throbbing nipple. His hard teeth nipped at it lightly, making her draw in a sharp breath of unexpected pleasure, and she moved beneath him in instinctive invitation, offering him the succulent fruit to taste and devour—and at last he drew it into his mouth, suckling at it with a deep, sweet rhythm that pulsed through her, sparking white fire into her brain.

He lifted his head, laughing in gentle teasing at the wantonness of her response. 'You're even sweeter in the flesh than in my dreams,' he murmured, his voice smoky from the fires in his eyes. 'Your body's so soft and warm and yielding—I could lie like this with you in my arms for the rest of eternity...'

And so could she, she mused, running her fingertips tentatively up over the hard curve of his shoulder, the rasping line of his jaw. She loved him, hopelessly, helplessly, even though she knew that for him eternity meant probably no more than this one night—maybe a few more if she was lucky. And then she would be left to face her loneliness again, all the more acute from having known this one brief interlude of heaven.

He took her fingers, kissing each of the tips in turn, and then his mouth came down to claim hers again in a kiss that was deep and tender, demanding all she had to give. And she surrendered herself to it totally, all her senses focused on the touch, the taste, the scent of him. The past, the future, everything but this exquisite present had faded into oblivion; there was nothing beyond the shadowed fringes of the pool of light that surrounded them, no sound but their own ragged breathing and the soft patter of the rain on the roof.

His hand was stroking in slow, lazy circles over the smooth curve of her stomach, and she sensed his intent as it moved lower, to slip beneath the fine, sheer lace of her briefs, easing them gently down until they slipped over her ankles and he tossed them aside. And then she felt his hand move back up; his touch was as light as a butterfly's wing, just one fingertip stroking smoothly, rhythmically over the satiny skin of her inner thighs as he gently coaxed them apart.

Trembling slightly, she offered no resistance; even in her dreams, nothing had prepared her for this. He had lifted his head again, and she knew that he was watching her as she lay naked in his arms, quivering at every caress, every exquisite response reflected in her face. Liquid heat was pooling in her belly and she turned her face into his chest, her cheek resting against the soft resilience of male muscle over hard bone as she breathed the musky scent of his skin.

Slowly, deliberately, he let his finger brush through the soft crown of curls at the crest of her thighs. She dragged in a long, shuddering breath, parting them wider, tension coiling inside her. He paused, laying tender kisses across her eyelids and the curve of her cheekbone, delaying the moment into an attenuated torment that had her twisting in voluptuous agony.

And then at last she felt the sweet intimacy of his touch against the pleats of delicate crimson flesh between. A shudder of pure ecstasy shivered through her, curling her spine as he began an erotic discovery, exploring the soft velvet crease to find the tiny seed-pearl hidden within, the tender focus of all her sizzling nerve-endings, arousing it with his sensual expertise until she was sobbing with pleasure, awash with the golden heat coursing through her veins.

'Georgia . . .' Her name was a whispered breath on his lips. He shifted his weight to lie above her, easing himself gently between her thighs. Her eyes fluttered open to gaze up at him. 'I'll try not to hurt you,' he promised with cherishing concern. 'If I do, I'll stop.'

'No . . .' She reached up, wrapping her arms around his neck to draw him down to her. 'Don't stop.'

And in fact she barely noticed the fleeting stab of pain as he entered her; her body welcomed it as the price of finally knowing this one moment of total, perfect unity. Holding him, both of them lying still as they let the sensations fill them, she could sense the restrained power in his hard-muscled body, sense the physical control that was holding it in check. If all that power were to be unleashed ...

Very slowly, she let one fingertip trail along the length of his spine. A warning tremor ran through him, deliciously dangerous, and she heard his sharp intake of breath. 'Georgia ... be careful,' he growled, tension straining his voice.

She laughed, seductively defiant. 'I'm not afraid of you,' she taunted in a tremulous whisper that somehow belied her bold words. 'Make love to me properly.'

His eyes glinted with warm approval. 'All right.' He chuckled, low and huskily. 'If you're sure that's what you want ...'

She gasped in shock as he thrust into her, deep and hard, and then drew back to do it again. He had slid his hand beneath her, lifting her against him, schooling her to his rhythm so that she met each movement, deepening the penetration, and she clung to his shoulders, her spine arching beneath him as she surrendered herself totally to his fierce demand.

Their bodies were swiftly slicked with a fine film of sweat, their breathing ragged; it was an explosion of pure, primitive pleasure, feverish and hungry, an elemental force fiercer than the thunderstorm that had brought them here. He gave her no respite but she wanted none—she had asked for this, and she wanted to feel the whole experience. It might be the only time in her life ...

And then at last, with a deep, volcanic tremor, he let go his breath in a harsh sigh and collapsed into her arms, his weight crushing her into the soft straw palliasse. A wave of pure tenderness swept through her and she stroked his hair, amazed at the weakness of that powerful body, every ounce of its strength spent.

She could stay like this for the rest of eternity—in this blissful state between dreams and waking, her body aching with the deep, warm satisfaction that at last she knew what it was like to surrender herself totally to the man she loved. But it was only a few moments before he stirred, and with a small grunt of contentment he shifted his weight, drawing her over to lie in his arms.

She lifted her head to look down at him—to find him smiling, his expression one of unmistakably smug satisfaction; he had won his bet. Suddenly the magic that had allowed her to step outside of herself was gone, and all the old tensions came flooding back. Humiliation stung her vulnerable heart, but she had learned long ago to keep fighting, even when she was hurting most. Pushing herself out of his arms, she sat up on the edge of the bed.

'Where do you think you're going, Blondie?' he enquired, his voice laced with lazy mockery.

'Anywhere... Nowhere,' she snapped angrily. There was nowhere she could go, lost in the middle of the moors on a night like this.

He laughed, reaching out to draw her back down onto the bed. 'You can't run away from me this time,' he taunted. 'And there are no great big beefy bodyguards to beat me up for you. I intend to make love to you all night.'

'What for?' she demanded bitterly. 'You only needed to do it once to win your damned bet.'

His eyes lit with comprehension. 'Ah, so that's what's bugging you...'

'Yes, that's what's bugging me,' she countered, rubbing her hand fiercely across her eyes to brush away the unwanted tears. 'And don't try denying it now, or making excuses, because I don't want to listen.'

'Well, you *are* going to listen,' he insisted, easily overcoming her attempts to escape from him. With a gentleness that contrasted strikingly with the strength with which he was holding her, he brushed the tears from her cheeks. 'First, I'm going to say I'm sorry. I know I should never have let that creep get to me the way he did, but the way he was talking about you made me want to smash his face to a pulp. Which would have spoilt the excellent decoration you put on it before—a lovely aim, that. Remind me never to argue with you when you're holding a horsewhip.'

Her narrowed eyes glittered warily up at him, but she stilled her useless struggles. The thought of him hitting Nigel on her behalf *was* rather beguiling.

'It was the last thing I wanted, to let you be the subject of a lot of unpleasant gossip,' he murmured, his soft voice infiltrating behind her defences. 'But I never intended to win the bet on a cheap score—I was playing for much higher stakes. I just wanted to see the creep's face when I collected my winnings—on our return from our honeymoon.'

Her eyes widened in stunned amazement. 'Our...honeymoon...?'

'That's what I said.' He laughed in wry self-mockery. 'This may be something of a back to front way of going about it, but I'm asking you to marry me.'

He had loosened his hold on her, and she sat up abruptly. 'You're crazy!' she protested in heated agitation. 'I've never heard such a ridiculous thing in my life!'

'Oh?' There was a warning hint of danger in his query. 'Why is it ridiculous?'

'Well, because... You don't love me, for a start.'

'Oh, did I forget to mention that?' he teased, sitting up and drawing her into his lap. 'I fell in love with you... Let me see, I think it was about the first time I kissed you. Though it could have been even earlier than that— it could have been the second you opened your eyes and looked up at me, an angry, frightened, vulnerable little mermaid. You knocked me clean off my feet—and by the time I came to my senses you'd vanished into the night like a dream.'

His breath was warm against her cheek, his voice low and persuasive. 'I couldn't get you out of my mind—I had to try and find you, even though it seemed hopeless. I couldn't believe my luck when I spotted you at that fancy charity bash in London—until I saw you with a million bucks' worth of rocks around your throat.'

'And, like a typical sexist, you assumed some man had given them to me in exchange for my favours,' she spat at him, jerking her head away. 'Very flattering.'

'Point taken,' he conceded equably. 'I've never seemed to be much good at thinking straight when I'm around you.' He put his hand beneath her chin, turning her face up to his. 'Are you going to hold that against me?'

She hesitated, uncertain of what to say. Why was he claiming all this now? Did he really expect her to believe that he was in love with her? But when he was looking at her like that, with that special, warm, intimate smile, she could believe almost anything.

'So?' he queried softly. 'Are you going to give me an answer?'

'I . . . I don't know,' she stammered. 'I . . . think I need a . . . little more time.'

'All right,' he conceded, his hand stroking gently along the line of her jaw and into her hair, drawing her closer. 'But perhaps I can try . . . a little persuasion.'

His mouth closed over hers, warm and soft, gently coaxing her lips apart. She knew she ought to resist, ought to try to clear her mind to think through the implications of what he had said, but the slow, sweet seduction of his kiss was luring her back into that world of languorous pleasure and dark forgetfulness, where all thoughts of tomorrow and beyond ceased to have any meaning.

Her head tipped back into the crook of his arm as the kiss deepened, his tongue tracing over the delicate membranes of her lips and swirling into every secret corner of her mouth, rekindling the lingering embers of arousal. Her body was already finely attuned to his touch, melting into a helpless response as he began to caress her. She moaned softly, moving against him, her breasts aching for his touch, her nipples already exquisitely tender, so that the merest brush of his fingertips sent sparks of fire into her brain.

But this time she wanted to touch him too. The maleness of his body fascinated her—the contrast to her own slender femininity. Leaning over him, she liked the way he could lift her so easily, as if she weighed virtually nothing. She wanted to run her hands over his warm, firm flesh, to feel the hard contour of muscle over bone, to trace her fingers through the rough hair that was scattered across his chest and then down in a narrow line over the lean plane of his stomach—down to...

'Go on,' he urged gently. 'There's nothing to be shy about now.'

Tentatively, she put out her hand and stroked one finger along the hard length of his manhood. The deep tremor of response that shimmered through him transmitted its charged vibrations through her own body, and she smiled down at him, delighted in the knowledge that she could give him some of the pleasure that he had given her.

'Show me how,' she whispered.

He laughed in rich satisfaction, moving to lay her down on her back again. 'I will,' he promised. 'But not tonight. Tonight I'm a little too...close to the edge. There are a thousand things I want to teach you, but we have plenty of time—all the time in the world. Tonight can only be a very brief introduction—a taste of what's to come...'

He was kneeling over her, holding her hands back above her head, so that her breasts were lifted invitingly to his caress, and as he bent over them, his hot, rough tongue lapping first at one succulent pink peak then the other, she whimpered with sweet anticipation, sheer ecstasy.

In was a torment of pleasure, driving her almost to the point of delirium as he nibbled and sucked at her tender nipples, drawing them deep into his mouth in an erotic tug that made her cry out on a sobbing breath, fire coursing through her veins. She had thought last time that she could go no higher, but already she was soaring in a giddy vortex, her body awash with blissful sensation, her mind lost in a whirlpool of incandescent flame.

She sensed him moving, uttered a weak cry of protest, but he mocked her with teasing laughter. 'Don't worry, sweet little wanton—you'll enjoy this even more.' His hand slid down to part her slender thighs, intimately exploring the moist, delicate folds of velvet between, the pad of his thumb caressing the throbbingly sensitive nub of pleasure as his fingers dipped deep inside her, stretching her deliciously.

She moaned softy, warmth pooling in the pit of her stomach like a crucible for the molten gold that was flowing through her veins, melting her bones. And then he bent his head, his kisses tracing a leisurely path from the ripe swell of her breasts down over her smooth stomach and into the crest of crisp, curling hair at the cleft of her thighs. She caught her breath in shock, her eyes flying open to meet the wicked glint in his as he snaked out his tongue and lapped it languorously over that dainty seed-pearl, swirling around it until the sizzling charge shot through her, curling her spine in rapturous response.

This time when he took her it was with a smooth, powerful thrust, and as she reached up to wrap her arms around him he lifted her onto his lap, moving her to his will, his mouth suckling at her aching breasts as her head tipped back to arch them invitingly towards him. The heated rhythm was sending quivering tremors through her body, searing her brain, as the glow of the storm-lamp cast the shadow of their erotic dance against the wall.

It was a long, slow languorous loving, warm and sensuous, wild and frenzied. Their bodies totally in tune, they moved to the beat of some primeval drum, possessing and possessed, driven by forces as old as time. And as Jake finally laid her back on the bed, his convulsive movements building to a crescendo as he thrust into her with deep, powerful strokes that seemed to reach into the very core of her body, she felt an answering tension building inside her, like the shimmering heat before a thunderstorm, coiling tighter and tighter...until with a shock like a stab of lightning it exploded through her, leaving her weak and exhausted, curled up in Jake's arms, her cheek resting contentedly against the warmth of his chest as she listened to the deep beat of his heart, slowly returning to its normal even pace.

CHAPTER TEN

GEORGIA stood at the window of her office, high above
the City, gazing pensively down over the jumble of roofs
below her. From this height, the view was both pan-
oramic and strangely intimate—she could see into all
those little tucked-away corners that were hidden from
the street: the spires of churches that had escaped both
the Blitz and the developers, the unexpected patches of
green.

The early-morning sun was reflecting brilliantly back
at her from the windows of one of the other skyscrapers,
making her eyes water, and she turned away, blinking
back the tears. That was all they were—a natural reaction to the dazzle of light. She wasn't crying.

It was forty-eight hours now since she had woken in
that rough shepherd's hut up on the Northumberland
moors, to find that the thunderstorm had passed, leaving
a fading mist that drew each hill as a separate silhouette,
layering one behind the other into the distance. It had
been a breathtaking sight, but she had been in no mood
to appreciate it.

The clear light of day had chased away the magical
spell of the night, leaving her with nothing but a handful
of anxieties and uncertainties; she had dressed quickly
in her rough-dried clothes before Jake had stirred, afraid
of the prickling awareness of her own vulnerability. By
the time he woke she had been able to force herself to
face him with a least a semblance of her usual cool composure, though she had not quite been able to bring
herself to meet his eyes.

Leaving the refuge of the hut, they had discovered that if they had walked just a little further the previous night they would have reached a farmhouse, tucked into a fold of the hills. The farmer and his wife had been startled to see them, so far from the beaten track and looking so bedraggled, but they had made them very welcome with a huge farmhouse breakfast, and had let them use the phone to call the police.

The drama of the subsequent events had been a welcome distraction from the awkwardness between them. The police had descended on the quarry to find all three kidnappers—the third had just returned and released his mates, and they had presumably been sitting around planning what to do next—and after a short chase across the moors, involving four-wheel drive vehicles and a helicopter, they had been caught.

After that there had been the long process of making their statements to the police. She had finally managed to get away late in the afternoon, while Jake was being still interviewed, flying down to London by helicopter for a hastily convened meeting with the takeover panel to persuade them to suspend trading in Geldard's shares when the markets opened after the Bank Holiday.

She had been at least partially successful; they had granted her twenty-four hours—enough time to put together the financial backing to buy up as many of Geldard's shares as she could. It might not be enough to prevent a severe slide in the share price once the embargo was lifted, but she hoped to avoid total disaster.

Meanwhile, she had been careful to ensure that her staff were aware that she was not available to take calls from Mr Morgan. She knew that it could be no more than a temporary respite—she wouldn't be able to go on avoiding him for ever—but she needed time—time to sort out the tangle of unfamiliar emotions, time to decide whether she could really trust her own heart.

Moving restlessly over to her desk, she sat down and tried to focus her attention on the latest stock market analysis, but her mind was distracted. When the door opened quietly she didn't even need to look up—her finely attuned instincts had already warned her who it was.

'Good morning. I thought I might find you here.'

'Not a particularly difficult deduction,' she responded coolly. 'This *is* still my office.'

He let the door swing shut behind him, moving across the room to perch on the edge of her desk. 'I gather Falcon have withdrawn their bid.'

She conceded a slight shrug of her slender shoulders. 'Inevitably. And there are two vacancies on the board— my doting uncles have offered their resignations. Apparently they were both involved—Juan promised the chairmanship to each of them privately, and they were both so warped by their pathological envy of each other that they fell right into his trap.'

Jake smiled in wry humour. 'The fools. Where are they now?'

'I believe the euphemism is "helping the police with their enquiries".'

'Serves them right,' he mused grimly. 'Still, perhaps it will be some comfort to them to hear that the débâcle has also had some unpleasant consequences for your playboy friend.'

'Oh?' In spite of herself, she was interested.

'Apparently he's announced that he's retiring to one of his more remote estates to concentrate on farming, and handing over control of all his assets to César.'

She stared at him in blank astonishment. '*What? Juan* retiring to his estates? But...'

'A bloodless coup,' he surmised with a dry smile. 'I see the hand of Dona Elena behind it—she's the one with the powerful political connections, and she's been tiring of his little games for a long time. I think she saw this as an opportunity to finally put him in his place.'

'Well, at least it means I don't have to worry about him any more,' Georgia mused. 'But it's still—'

She was interrupted by a tap on the door, and Bernard Harrison appeared. 'Ah, Georgia, you're here. And Mr Morgan—how very good to see you.' Georgia couldn't help thinking his welcome to Jake was just a trifle over-enthusiastic. 'I thought you'd like to have the latest update from the Tokyo Exchange as soon as it came in.' He handed her a sheet of computer printout, covered with rows of tiny figures. 'Congratulations. I admit I was a little worried that with the market there opening ahead of ours there might be an outbreak of panic selling as soon as Falcon's shares were released—I should have known you'd be ready to forestall it.'

Georgia was frowning as she studied the rows of figures on the paper; Bernard seemed to have been addressing his remarks to Jake rather than her, and as her brain began to make sense of the evidence in front of her she lifted her eyes slowly to meet that dark gaze. 'You've bought up Falcons's shares!' she breathed, her anger seething. 'Of all the sneaking, deceitful, underhand...'

He silenced her with a look that reminded her of the company secretary's presence. 'Excuse us for a moment, Bernard,' he requested of that startled gentleman, ushering him swiftly but politely out of the door. 'I think there's about to be a blood-letting.' He closed the door and turned back to Georgia with a mockingly expectant smile.

'You...*bastard*!' she threw at him furiously. 'You were planning this all along, weren't you? You must have jumped in the minute the embargo was lifted. I never thought even you would sink so low as to use the Tokyo Exchange to get in ahead of me...'

He held up his hand to stem her flow. 'Hold on! You think I was planning some kind of back door takeover of my own? Not guilty. As it happens, I always use Tokyo—in case you hadn't noticed, it's rather more convenient for Sydney than London. What's happened is really very simple. Like Bernard, I've been concerned about what could happen if and when de Perez dumped his shares on the market—a bundle like that hitting the floor all in one go could send the price into free-fall, and heaven only knows who might pick them up. I knew you wouldn't be able to afford to put up an adequate defence, so I left standing instructions with my broker to buy as soon as they hit one-eighty. Apparently he's done his job...'

'Which let you buy us up on the cheap!'

'I have no intention of buying you up,' he rapped back, holding onto his temper with evident difficulty. 'If you look a little more carefully at those figures, you'll see that I've limited my overall holding to twenty percent.'

'Oh, yes I *had* noticed that,' she countered bitterly. 'And that's supposed to make me feel better, is it? Having you hovering there behind me, waiting to pounce whenever it suits you?'

'I told you, I'm not planning to launch a takeover. In fact, between us we now have a majority holding—overall control. That's what you wanted, isn't it?'

'Not if I have to rely on you for it!'

'You still don't trust me?'

'Trust you? I'd rather trust a rattlesnake!'

'I see.' They had been confronting each other eyeball-to-eyeball across her desk, their voices steadily rising, but suddenly his manner changed. He stepped back, shrugging his wide shoulders in that characteristic gesture of unconcern. 'Well, if you're not ready to trust me, you certainly aren't ready to marry me,' he stated, very quietly but with chilling finality. 'If you should ever decide to change your mind, you'll know where to find me.'

She stared after him, stunned by the speed with which the explosive tension between them had fizzled away, leaving an empty void. He had turned his back on her and walked away, but just as the door was closing she found her voice to yell, 'Don't hold your breath!' The only response was a mocking laugh.

She sat back heavily, struggling for breath against the tight constriction in her chest. He had gone—he had just walked away, and she knew he wouldn't come back. How could he do that if he loved her? Or had it all been a lie, just as she had suspected all along? Had he never really wanted to marry her after all...?

Tears welled into her eyes, too many to hold back, spilling over her cheeks. She had known it wasn't real—of course she had; but it was cruel of him to snatch it away so soon. He could have let the dream last just a little longer.

The crowd was cheering wildly as the horses came round the last bend, the leaders bunched on the rails, their hooves thundering on the springy green turf as they galloped down the home straight to the finish. Georgia watched through her binoculars, an odd little thud in her heart. One horse had its nose in front—an unusual palomino, chestnut-gold, with a pale blonde mane and tail.

'Come on, Blondie,' someone close to her shrieked. 'That's the girl!'

Georgia drew in a long, shuddering breath. She wished the pretty mare no ill, but as urgently as her neighbour was urging her on to win she was wishing one of the others would overtake her. She hadn't heard that Jake was here, but the fear that there was even the remotest chance that she might have to present him with the winner's cup was enough to make her heart pound and her knees feel weak.

It was almost three weeks since he had walked away from her—the bleakest three weeks of her life. She had thought she knew what loneliness was, but she hadn't even scratched the surface of it before—it was a deep, dark, aching pit where not one single ray of sunlight could penetrate. At times she almost wished she had never met him—but that would mean that she wouldn't have had that night on the moors, the one thing she could cling to in her memories . . .

A loud roar told her that the race was over, and she realised that through the fine veil of tears that had misted her eyes she had missed the actual finish. 'Who won?' she enquired diffidently.

'Blondie! Come on, the jockeys will be weighing in, and then it'll be time to present the cup.'

The Geldard Cup was a beautiful thing of chased silver, with an engraved design of graceful horses racing around its bowl. Since her grandfather had instigated it, some twenty years ago, it had become one of the high-lights of the September race meeting at Ascot.

It was as if she was in a kind of trance as she allowed herself to be ushered down to the winners' enclosure, protected from the milling crowds by her attentive entourage. Would Jake be there? Somehow she was sure that he wasn't—surely if he was that close to her, she would have sensed it? But she couldn't escape from a vague sense that *something* was about to happen. Maybe it was just the thought of meeting the horse he had named after her, the horse he had staked in his arrogant as-surance that he could get her into bed.

The long, hot, glorious summer, so untypical of English summers, had lingered on into September. The sky was a clear, perfect blue, dusted with a few cotton-puff clouds, and there was just a hint of gold rusting the leaves of the tall trees on the edge of the course. The crowd parted to let her through into the small enclosed circle where the presentation would take place, then pressed in behind her again, craning towards the television cameras, eagerly hoping their faces would show up on countless television screens around the country.

Georgia was glad of the shelter of the wide brim of her chic hat, perfectly toned with the glowing aquamarine of her silk suit. She would have preferred not to be at the centre of so much attention, but there was no way she could avoid it. At least she could console herself that the real centre of attention was the lively young horse, still prancing as she was led round the ring, as if knowing that she had done well.

Blondie... It had infuriated her when he had called her that, but now she would have given almost anything to have him come up behind her, slide his arms around her waist and whisper the name in her ear... But he wouldn't come, and she had to hold herself erect, smiling pleasantly as she exchanged a few words with the trainer and the jockey, handing them their cheques and medals.

It always struck her as a little unfair that the ones who did all the work got only medals—and the poor horse who ran her heart out had to make do with a red rosette pinned to her bridle—while the owner, who did nothing but put up the money, took home the cup. It had been brought out of its box and was gleaming beautifully in the sun as the television camera focused down on it, and Georgia glanced around to see who was going to receive it on Jake's behalf.

'Afternoon, Georgie.' She glanced up in blank surprise as the Honourable Nigel Woodvine stepped forward, taking her hand and leaning forward to kiss her on the cheek. 'Knew I'd win the cup this year—thanks to you. Nice little filly, ain't she? I've got very high hopes of her.'

'She's *yours*?' Georgia's head seemed to swim; she barely even noticed as the Geldard Cup was placed into her hands and she automatically presented it to Nigel, smiling for the television cameras. 'But...I thought...'

'I won my bet, didn't I?' Nigel asserted smugly. 'Did you think I'd call it off? I don't back out of certainties, sweetie—and I really enjoyed wiping the smile off that stupid, jumped-up Aussie's face. And now he's gone how's about you and me doing a little serious celebrating tonight? What do you say?'

She shook her head dumbly, turning away from him—and found Robin Rustrom-Smith at her side. He took her elbow, drawing her a little away from the group now posing for photographs and interviews with the television presenter. 'You all right, Georgie?' he queried in concern.

'Yes, I...' She frowned, staring at Nigel. 'I don't understand. Jake told Nigel he'd won the bet?'

'Well, yes...' Robin looked a little perplexed. 'Are you saying...he didn't?'

She shook her head. 'No, he didn't. Jake won.'

'Well, I'm damned!' As the implications of her words sank in Robin blushed, flustered and embarrassed. 'What the devil...? Well, I...always did think it was a pretty rum sort of bet. Frankly, I'm not surprised he chuffed it—seemed a decent sort of chap. As a matter of fact, he asked me to give you this.' Fumbling in his pocket, he took out a small key and put it into her hands. 'He said if I didn't hear anything from him before, I was to give it to you this afternoon.'

She blinked, looking down at the key in confusion. It was a safe-deposit key. 'What...?'

'Here's the number,' Robin added, opening his wallet and handing her a slip of paper. 'Don't lose it.'

* * *

The safe-deposit clerk inserted the key Robin had given her, and his own, into the locks on the box and opened the door, sliding out the tray inside. He set it down carefully on the wooden table in the middle of the security room and politely withdrew.

Georgia opened the lid of the tray, her heart thumping. Inside were several thick folds of paper and she took them out, opening them one by one: the deeds of her house, so recently sold, though the copy of the Land Registry Certificate attached showed it as still belonging to her; the papers for the *Geldard Star*, also still bearing her name, and a transfer certificate for shares in Geldard's in her favour, for fifteen percent of the total share issue.

Her mouth dry, she stared at the pile of documents. There was no note, no explanation—nothing to tell her why he had done it. She couldn't even begin to add up the amount of money the documents represented— though to him it was probably no more than a couple of months' turnover.

Was it his way of apologising for that stupid bet? Or was he telling her he washed his hands of her—the most expensive kiss-off in history?

The tray wasn't empty yet—at the bottom was a velvet box, long and flat, and very familiar. Her hands were trembling as she picked it up and opened it; the Geldard diamonds sparkled up at her, taking the light from the fluorescent strip above her head and transforming into a million points of fire.

Damn him—he was challenging her to trust her instincts. If she refused this outrageous gesture—or, worse still, accepted it and did nothing—she would be drawing a very final line beneath their relationship. But if she contacted him how did she know he wouldn't reject her? How did she know he had meant it when he told her he loved her?

* * *

A flotilla of white yachts were scudding across the sparkling blue waters of Sydney Harbour; Jake stood at the window of his office on the twenty-third floor of the Morgan building, in the heart of the downtown business district, gazing absently out at the spectacular view. His thoughts were far away—ten thousand miles away, to be exact.

Damn that woman—he had been content enough with his life until he had met her. Happy, even—who wouldn't be? He had it made—even if he had begun to think that he had used up all his share of good luck with his meteoric business success, and that if he ever wanted to marry and have kids he would be condemned to settle for a choice between some money-grubbing harpy or a feather-brained bimbo who gawked at him in awe and substituted inane giggling for intelligent conversation.

With a sigh he turned away from the window and moved back to his desk, flicking the intercom to speak to his secretary—after a number of disastrous experiences with the usual female variety, in a range of ages, he had finally settled for a man. 'Chris—I need the papers on that road-widening scheme in Wahroonga. I might take a look at them over the weekend.'

'I thought you were going fishing?'

'Yeah, well . . . I can read and fish, can't I?'

'You can,' the young man conceded with easy humour. 'But it's usually best to do one or the other. Hey, come on, boss, what are you doing working over Labour Day weekend? It's a holiday. Even *you* have to take a break now and then.'

'When I need your advice on my health, I'll ask for it!' Jake snapped with uncharacteristic impatience. 'Just fetch me those papers and mind your own damned business.'

'OK, OK . . .'

Jake threw himself into the big, deep, leather executive chair, swinging it back and stretching his arms behind his head. What the hell was the matter with him, snapping at people like that? Maybe Chris was right, and he needed to make the effort to relax a little. He could do with a decent night's sleep too—something he had never had a problem with until recently.

By the time his secretary came into the room with the report he had asked for, he was ready to offer a wry apology. 'That's OK,' Chris responded with a shrug. 'It's not like I was going to hand my notice in or anything. Seems to me maybe you ought to give her a call.'

'Who?' Jake demanded, instantly aggressive again.

'The dame that's been bugging you ever since you got back from England. The trouble with you is you've never had trouble with women before, so you're not equipped to handle it. You're sitting here trying to play Mr Cool, and it's doing your head in.'

'Oh? And you're some sort of expert, are you?' Jake retorted, a sardonic note in his voice.

'On women trouble? I'm the oracle. I've been dumped by more women than you've had hot dinners.'

'I wasn't dumped!'

'So what's your problem? Pick up the phone. OK, so it's the middle of the night over there—well, five in the morning anyway. But what the hell? Maybe she can't sleep either.'

Jake regarded the telephone on his desk in wry contemplation. Chris was right—it would be so easy to call her, just to hear her voice . . . But he shook his head—he had never been the first to crack in any deal, and he wasn't going to make a start now. 'No—it's her move. Give me that report, Chris, and then you might as well get off. Have a nice weekend.'

'Same to you,' the younger man responded with a sympathetic grin. 'Good fishing.'

Left alone, Jake rose restlessly to his feet again, pacing across to the window and resting his hands high against the cool glass. He hadn't realised Chris had guessed what was wrong with him—he had flattered himself that he wasn't making it obvious.

Hell, this was crazy! All this hassle over one dumb broad? Weren't there enough women right here in town? Maybe he'd call up Nicole, take her out to dinner—or Bianca...

Or maybe he wouldn't. Chris had been right, he acknowledged with a touch of bitter self-mockery—he wasn't used to having trouble with women, and he was finding it a lot harder to handle than he'd expected.

Shaking his head in weary exasperation, he picked up the thick file and dropped it into his briefcase, and then, with a last glance around the office to check that everything was secure, he locked the door behind him and took the executive lift down to the basement car park.

The sleek black hand-built Lister he had imported from England turned startled heads as it growled menacingly up out of the underground car park—people always looked at it as if they expected to see Lucifer himself at the wheel. But even in the heavy rush-hour traffic it was beautifully behaved—though intimidating enough to persuade every other driver on the road to give him priority.

It didn't take him too long to get out onto the wide freeway, heading out towards South Head. Maybe one day maybe he'd buy a house out here, he mused, sparing a fleeting glance for one or two of the big white mansions in their leafy gardens as he swept past them—until now he'd always found the small apartment above the office and his boat quite sufficient, but lately he'd found himself wanting something more out of life than the rootless existence that had served him for near enough the past twenty years.

The Kestrel was waiting for him, gleaming white in the spring sunshine, stocked up and ready to sail the moment he stepped aboard. He handed over his briefcase to the steward, and went up to join his captain in the wheelhouse. The powerful sixteen-cylinder twin diesel engines almost seemed to purr as the sleek aluminum hull sliced through the warm crystal waters, and the bank of small screens along the dashboard behind the wheel glowed pale green as they updated every detail of position, radar picture and depth-sounding.

'Hi, Pete—how's it going?' he remarked, strolling over to take a look at the navigation chart laid out on the table beside the helm seat.

'Fine, mate,' the captain responded, with the same easy camaraderie. 'Want to take the wheel?'

Jake shook his head. Was it his imagination, or were his crew giving him odd looks too? Did the whole damned state know what had been going on? 'No—you take her out. I think I'll go get myself a drink.'

He strolled down to the saloon, something of the impatience of a caged tiger in his stride. Maybe once they got out onto the open ocean he would feel better—and the prospect of some good deep-sea fishing always improved his temper. He poured himself a thick slug of brandy and sat down, lounging at full length on one of the hide sofas.

The trouble was, this room was too full of memories now—memories of *her*. She had lain there, on that sofa opposite him... Damn, the images were so real he could almost smell her perfume...

It was at that point that he noticed the envelope on the table—a plain brown envelope, with no address or stamp on it. He leaned forward, frowning, and picked it up. Opening it, he drew out the papers inside, they were the registration papers for that pretty palomino filly, made out once again in his name.

'Well, I'll be...' Rising to his feet, he looked around the room. There was no other clue... but, following his instincts, he walked over and slowly pushed open the door to the master state-room.

She was sitting on the bed, cocooned in his wine-red silk sheets—all he could see was the top of her blonde head. But as he closed the door quietly behind him she peeped up, those big blue eyes gazing up at him, wide and uncertain.

He took his time, taking another sip of the brandy before he spoke. 'So—you finally made it, then?'

'Uh-huh.' She lowered the sheet to her chin.

He held up the registration papers. 'What's this about?' he enquired.

'I... bought her back for you. After all, you won the bet.'

'So I did.' He was beginning to wonder what she was doing, wrapped up in that sheet. But after she had come all this way, the least he could do was go along with whatever little game she wanted to play. 'I take it Robin gave you the... er... item I left with him?' he enquired cordially.

'He did.' She chuckled with laughter, soft and low and startling sexy. 'Thank you. As a matter of fact, I'm wearing the diamonds...' She slowly spread wide her arms, laying aside the sheet. 'Do you still think they go with my eyes?'

She certainly was wearing the diamonds—and nothing else. They sparkled against her creamy-gold skin, drawing the eye—but not so much as the delightful curve of her breasts, firm and ripe, pertly tipped with pink, lifting invitingly as she raised her arms languidly above her head. Nor so much as the cute curve of her stomach, downy-soft as a peach. And not nearly as much as the soft crown of golden curls at the cleft of her slender thighs as she provocatively curled her long legs beneath her.

Raw desire cut through him like a knife, taking his breath away. She was offering him everything he had asked for—much, much more than her beautiful naked body. She had come halfway round the world to him, willing to take a risk that he knew scared the hell out of her, willing to trust that her damned grandfather had been wrong after all. It was there in her eyes, an edge of anxiety, of aching vulnerability, and it melted his heart.

'It took you long enough to come round to this,' he growled thickly, moving across the room, setting the brandy glass and the registration papers down on the bedside table and starting to unfasten his shirt.

'I know. I'm...sorry.' Those clear blue eyes looked up at him, misted with tears that he wanted to kiss away. 'Forgive me?'

Joy surged in his heart and he sat down on the side of the bed, catching her in his arms and drawing her onto his lap, laughing, loving the feel of her lithe, slender body in his arms, so sweetly naked, loving the knowledge that this smart, sassy woman, who could run a major public company and scare the living daylights out of most men he knew, had chosen to give herself exclusively to him.

'I'll only forgive you on the condition that you never keep me waiting again,' he growled, almost angry with her for the strain she had put him through over the past few weeks. 'Whenever I want you, you be there—on the double. Right?'

'Right.'

'No ifs, buts or maybes?' he challenged fiercely.

She shook her head, her eyes laughing up at him. 'None at all. Mind you,' she added on a note of impish mischief, one dainty fingertip trailing a meandering path through the crisp hair on his chest, 'we could be in danger of bankruptcy if we're not careful. My business is in Europe and yours is down here. How will we manage without neglecting one or the other?'

'We'll build one great big empire to straddle the world,' he declared, feeling as though with her at his side he could do anything. 'Morgan-Geldard.'

'Geldard-Morgan,' she contradicted him, just for the sake of it, her delicate mouth curving into a provocative smile.

'You want to argue about it?'

'No,' she purred, nestling against him in a way that drove every other thought from his brain. 'I didn't sit here getting goose-bumps for two hours just so we could talk business.'

'Goose-bumps?' He ran his hand down over her warm, silken skin, savouring its smooth contours and textures. 'I don't feel any goose-bumps.'

'They've gone now.'

She lifted her face to his, her soft lips parted in delicious temptation—a temptation he wasn't even going to try to resist. Her mouth was like honey, yielding beneath his, and he plundered its moist, warm depths with a fierce demand that he could no longer hold in check.

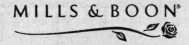

MILLS & BOON®

Next Month's Romances

♡

Each month you can choose from a wide variety of romance with Mills & Boon. Below are the new titles to look out for next month in our two new series Presents and Enchanted.

Presents™

TOO WISE TO WED?	Penny Jordan
GOLD RING OF BETRAYAL	Michelle Reid
THE SECOND MRS ADAMS	Sandra Marton
HONEYMOON FOR THREE	Sandra Field
THE UNEXPECTED FATHER	Kathryn Ross
RYAN'S RULES	Alison Kelly
SUBSTITUTE BRIDE	Angela Devine
THE DOMINANT MALE	Sarah Holland

Enchanted™

BRINGING UP BABIES	Emma Goldrick
FALLING FOR HIM	Debbie Macomber
SECOND-BEST WIFE	Rebecca Winters
THE BABY BATTLE	Shannon Waverly
HIS CINDERELLA BRIDE	Heather Allison
MISLEADING ENGAGEMENT	Marjorie Lewty
A ROYAL ROMANCE	Valerie Parv
LIVING WITH MARC	Jane Donnelly

Available from WH Smith, John Menzies, Volume One, Forbuoys, Martins, Woolworths, Tesco, Asda, Safeway and other paperback stockists.

GET 4 BOOKS AND A MYSTERY GIFT

FREE

Return this coupon and we'll send you 4 Mills & Boon Presents™ novels and a mystery gift absolutely FREE! We'll even pay the postage and packing for you.

We're making you this offer to introduce you to the benefits of Reader Service: FREE home delivery of brand-new Mills & Boon Presents novels, at least a month before they are available in the shops, FREE gifts and a monthly Newsletter packed with information.

Accepting these FREE books and gift places you under no obligation to buy, you may cancel at any time, even after receiving just your free shipment. Simply complete the coupon below and send it to:

MILLS & BOON® READER SERVICE, FREEPOST, CROYDON, SURREY, CR9 3WZ.

No stamp needed

Yes, please send me 4 free Mills & Boon Presents novels and a mystery gift. I understand that unless you hear from me, I will receive 6 superb new titles every month for just £2.10* each, postage and packing free. I am under no obligation to purchase any books and I may cancel or suspend my subscription at any time, but the free books and gift will be mine to keep in any case. (I am over 18 years of age)

P6LE

Ms/Mrs/Miss/Mr _____

Address _____

_____

_____ Postcode _____

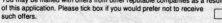

Temptation ®

What better way to celebrate *the* most romantic day of the year...

My Valentine

We're delighted to celebrate this day with a wonderful collection of four short stories. Written by popular Temptation authors, these stories capture the fun, fantasy and sizzle of February 14th.

Denim and Diamonds   *by Gina Wilkins*
The Valentine Raffle   *by Kristine Rolofson*
A Very Special Delivery   *by JoAnn Ross*
Valentine Mischief   *by Vicki Lewis Thompson*

Happy Valentine's Day!

Available: January 1997   **Price: £4.99**